# Dedication

My first novel is dedicated to my late auntie, Christine (Tina) Tatum Shelton. My auntie has always been my cheerleader. She introduced me to reading novels. She would buy novels and pass them to me after she read them first when I told her I enjoyed reading and that I write poems and kept a journal that I wrote in every day. She would say, "Keep it up baby and one day, you can be an author." She instilled writing & reading in me. She encouraged me to follow my dreams and in her words she would say, "Don't you ever let a motherfucker tell you what you can't do." I love and miss you auntie! Now both of our names are in print!

# Acknowledgments

First and foremost, I must thank God for blessing me with the gift of creativity. I've wanted to be an author since I was a child. Just when I thought I couldn't do it, the 4 people who encouraged me the most are my children; Shaneah, Shakerah, Stephan, Daniel Jr..(DJ) and my grandson Jaden. I want to thank you guys for having my back and telling me, "Mommy, it's never too late." I love you guys and I did this for you. Y'all are my everything and my reason for me to keep pushing.

I would also like to thank my mother, Phyllis Shelton Obery. Thank you for your continued love and support. Thank you for passing down your talents! You are also the reason for my gift. You are a talented woman and I love you! Now your name is in print! I got to give thanks to my sistas! My A1's from day one, Chante Collins, Shavonne Smith, and Shakira Chambers. You ladies are a true inspiration! These are three strong and beautiful women who I love like we are blood related. These ladies have encouraged and helped me in so many ways. I love you and thank you for your continued support. I would also like to thank my other three sisters, Pamela Rawls, Nikki Mathews, and Kalimah Farrakhan (Leemy), who have always supported me. Thank you ladies for listening to me vent and for encouraging me when I doubted myself and my abilities. Thank you for loving me and accepting me as I am. I love y'all! Y'all know we are going to have some haters!

Thanks to all of my family! You guys are my foundation and from where I stem. I love you guys always. I would like to thank my publisher, Ms. Jan'a Sullivan. Thank you for taking a chance on me and believing in me. Thank you for allowing me the platform to make my dreams come true. I really appreciate you. I can't and won't forget the one person, who gave it to me raw and kept it 100 with me. You have helped me tremendously and I am forever grateful. She motivated me when I needed it and told me not to give up. When I was doubting myself, she lifted me up and helped me push through. Thank you so much Ms. Jay Johnson! You rock girl! The entire MSP team; you guys are an inspiration. I someday hope to be just as great as you are. Keep writing. You give people like me reasons to keep pushing. Thank you! Last but not least, my daddy, Billy Obery, I hope you are grinning now daddy! I miss you so much! Thank you so much for showing me real true love. Continue to rest in peace.

Live, Love, Laugh, & WRITE!

Leshonda Obery

# Synopsis

Three best friends, Erica, Jaiden , and Me'asha, came from the hood and now own their own businesses. They vowed to escape the hood life of hustling, but find themselves thrown back in the game when Erica and Me'asha's criminal turned legit businessmen boyfriends, Jahmar and Tone get caught up with the feds. Unfortunately, everything ain't what it seems. At what cost are they willing to keep their men and eachother out of trouble? With secrets being revealed, will this cause rip between sisters? Best friends forced back into the game trying to be faithful to the men in their lives and faithful to themselves. Things get turnt…when the lies go beyond the streets.

# Slipped and Fell In Love With A Boss

## <u>Prologue</u>

"Babe, let me help you with that."

I'm sitting on the bed trying to unstrap my shoes, and here comes Jah looking sexy as hell. He sees me having a

hard time with my shoes, got on one knee and took my shoes off. Feeling

relieved to be sitting up I said, "Thank you baby." As he stood, I unfastened his belt and unbuttoned his pants. I

pulled them down and he stepped out of them. He looked at me in a drunken daze and said, "Tee, you forgot

something."

"Don't worry baby, I got you." I whispered.

He was looking at me like he wanted to fuck the shit out of me, but not yet; I needed something to drink. I had

cotton-mouth. "Jah, bring me a glass of water please." As he turned into the bathroom, I took my dress off and

sat on the edge of the bed. He handed me my water, I sipped it real slow and gave the glass back to him. When

he returned, I ordered him to stand in front of me. I took his draws off, grabbed his dick, and kissed the tip.

"Oh shit!" He moaned. I hadn't even done anything yet, but I know my mouth was warm. I kissed it again but

this time, I put his entire dick in my mouth. Licking and sucking that dick like I was never gonna do it again. I

grabbed his balls and played with them while I sucked that dick.

"Damn baby. You tryna kill a nigga." He said.

"No baby, I just wanna make you feel good."

I was returning the favor he showed me earlier. I pushed him back, stood up, turned him around and pushed him on the bed. I continued to suck his dick and in his drunk raspy voice he said, "Sit on it, baby! I want you to fuck me!" That was like music to my ears. I love when he talks like that to me. I straddled that dick and rode that shit like a professional horse rider. We were cumming together. He's screaming and I'm screaming. *This shit good as hell!* Then all of a sudden, I stopped and said, "Jah, you heard that?"

He was holding onto my wrist and said, "Yeah, but who the fuck is that this time of night?"

We got up and threw some clothes on and went downstairs. The closer we got, the louder the knocking became. Jah put on his hood voice and said, "Who the fuck is it?"

He looked at me and I'm over here a little scared.

"Newark Police!"

Oh shit! What the fuck??? Jah answered the door and standing there were five cops in the doorway. Before either of us could say anything, one of the cops asked, "Jahmar Morton?"

"Yes, how can I help you officer?" Jah said.

They pulled out a piece of paper and said, "Turn around sir."

"The fuck? What the fuck for?" Jah said. I saw the other officers getting nervous as they placed their hands on their guns. As soon as Jah started asking questions, things started getting tense; now I was getting nervous. The cop addressed Jah and said, "We have a warrant for your arrest. The charges are drug trafficking, and possession of narcotics with the intent to distribute, and two counts of first-degree murder. Again, Mr. Morton, turn around and place your hands behind your back. This can get real ugly real fast if you don't cooperate."

Jahmar turned around, looked me in my eyes and said, "Call Spaz now!"

All I'm thinking is WTF! I know better thanto question him now. I just looked at him and said,

"Ok baby. Call me and I'll come snatch you."

"Just call Spaz! I love you."

The officer handed me his card and said, "You can call the station in about 45 minutes to an hour and find out what his bail is or if there even is a bail."

This some straight up bullshit! I can't believe I'm in some bullshit I said I wanted no part of. How in the hell did I end up here? Oh I know, see what had happened was... Let me start from the beginning!

# Erica (Topaz)

I looked at the clock on the wall in my office and I realized that it was way past quitting time.

I hadn't even taken a lunch break. I'm so tired of punching a damn time clock and working

hard as hell. I'm damn near killing myself, and for what? A nice condo in the suburbs, some

fabulous shoes and clothes and a couple of nice pieces of jewelry, with no man to share it

with? I can't remember the last time I had a good fuck. Hell, I own so many fucking pleasure

toys, you'd think I owned a store. I remember when I used to get my fuck on. But since

working in my position as the editor-in-chief of The Voice, A monthly urban publication

or what my people call, "The Black Magazine",  I haven't had the time to meet any new

prospects. I remember when I use to think about having a husband and a family. Right

now, all I want is some meaningless mind blowing sex with a fine ass brother and no strings

attached. With my luck that, won't happen. The brothers can't help but get attached to me.

That's because my hotspot is the spot or so I've been told! I crack myself up sometimes but hell it's the truth.

Well let me get the hell outta here; a bitch tired. Just as I was locking up my office, who did I see grinning so

wide that I could feel that shit with my eyes closed?  Mr. Gordon, the president of 'The Voice.'

"Well Ms. Topaz, how are you this evening? I see we're burning that night oil, huh?"

"Good evening Mr. Gordon and yes. You know my work is never done."

I closed my office door and prepared myself for this drawn out conversation I'm about to have. As soon as I

closed the door, he started. "So, how are you enjoying your new position?" He asked.

The way he looked at me was like I was his prime rib dinner and he wanted to eat me up.

He wasn't that bad looking, he is high yellow, and stood about 5'8" tall, with a bald head, and green eyes. His eyebrows, eyelashes, and mustache, were all red! He looked like a human lion. Some women think he is the finest thing to walk the earth. He's cute but, not my type. I like my men big and black. With the way I'm feeling, even Mr. Gordon was starting to look good to me. I wonder if he got a big dick? When I tried to get a glimpse of his package, I think he caught me, because he shifted his position like he was giving me a better look.

"Ms. Topaz, are you ok?"

I blinked twice because I was stuck for a second.

"Yes, I'm fine. I'm just a little tired. And yes, I'm enjoying my new position, although it's taking a lot of my time." I said. So much I can't even get my fuck on. All I'm thinking is I want to fuck, but he still talking. "Well Ms. Topaz, I won't hold you up, you have a great night."

As he turned to walk away, I responded and checked his booty out. Not bad I thought.

"Good night, Mr. Gordon."

**✳✳✳✳**

That had to be the longest drive ever. I'm happy that I am finally home. As I pulled into my driveway, I saw that my foyer light was on. I wondered if I left it on or is there someone in there? I was paranoid as hell. I knew I shouldn't have smoked that blunt on the way home. In my younger years, I always said that I would never stop smoking. Here I am, a 35-year-old, professional woman, getting my smoke on. If the suits knew I smoked weed damn near every night, I wouldn't be in my new position. Hell, I wouldn't even have a job. Shiiid, that's what wraps up my day. It relaxes me from all the stresses of my day. Hell, it really enhances my creative side for real! I see things differently from a lot of people. That shit helped me get my new position. Whenever I worked from home, I came up with some of the best issues The Voice has ever published. Besides, you can take the girl out the hood, but you can't take the hood out the girl. Don't get it fucked up now, because I'm very intelligent and I'm good at what I do. I'm like a chameleon, I can change and adapt to any environment or situation. I can be a classy, businesswoman when I need to be. I can also be a hood bitch. Most people in the writing industry see me as a straightforward and classy businesswoman, while others see me as the bitch from the Pj's who now thinks she the shit! Which I am! Now, back to my house. Shit, let me think…. fuck it! I'm going in. I probably left the light on. If I didn't and someone is in there, that motherfucker about to catch some heat. I got some fire for that ass! Shiiiid I'm from the hood, I know what it is. So I took out my little .22 just in case. I though I was NPD, because I put the key in the door, unlocked it and then I kicked the shit in with my gun in position. I searched the house and felt like an idiot. That shit was funny as hell though. If someone had been watching me they'd be laughing at my high ass. That whole shit blew my high. So of course, I went into my stash. I rolled another one to smoke while I soaked in the tub. While I ran water in the tub, I sat on the edge of the bed and took a couple of pulls off my blunt. I dreaded listening to my messages. Lord knows I didn't wanna hear that not one man has called me for some ass! I guess they say, 'fuck Erica!' She always busy. This might just be my lucky night! I had four messages. The first one from, guess who? My momma, with her country accent.

*"Erica, this ya momma calling. I hope I'm not being a pest by calling you all the time. If you would just return my calls, I wouldn't have to call you so much, bye."*

I have to call my momma before she have the cops looking for me.

Next, *"Hey baby, long time no hear from. This Big Daddy, holla at cha boy when you get a chance. I'm going out of town for a few days and I wanted to see you."*

Now, Big Daddy is one of my old flings from my old neighborhood. Big Daddy was just that, "big." He didn't use to be so big, but now he's too big and I don't have time to be searching for his dick. It seems like the bigger he gets, the smaller his dick gets. I'm not that desperate. DELETE! Next…

*"Hey bitch, holla at cha girl. This is Jai, I wanna ask you something."*

Tajai Thomas, aka Jai, is one of two of my best friends. We grew up together with my other best friend, Mia. We are from the same housing projects of Newark, NJ; We're real tight and we've been friends for over 21 years. Jai owns her own boutique selling her hot originals and she's a celebrity stylist. A bitch is paid, too! She dresses all the celebrities for their parties and functions. Jai is still project-ish too, but hell, we all are. We have become successful, and stayed successful business women. Jai reminds me of a younger Angela Bassett. She's beautiful and she knows it. Jai always said that, I was the bitch who thinks I'm the shit, when in reality, I'm learning from her, the queen bitch! I love her like my blood sister. I wonder what she wants. I'll call her back as soon as I get settled. I know she got a story to tell.

Next and finally the last message.

*"Hey girl this is Mia, Holla at ya girl! I got some hot V.I.P passes to that new club on the strip."*

Now Mia, aka Me'asha Lawson, was always the one with the hook up. Even when we were growing up in The Pj's. She was always the one to go to for clothes, shoes, and bootleg cable, or burnt out cell phones. We don't do that shit no more, but the sista got connects! Mia is always trying different things to enhance her beauty. The woman is beautiful! She puts me in the mind of Halle Berry. She's just a little taller. The men be stalking her ass when we go out. The bitch can cook her ass off too! Even from way back then, she used to make up shit to cook. That's why it didn't surprise me when she opened her own restaurant. She now has a second location out in LA. Who knew that us three hood rats would become three very successful business women, with lots of legal chips! I figured I'd return my calls when I'm done relaxing in the tub. I put on some Will Downing, poured a couple of drops of cucumber melon oil in the tub and eased my body down slowly and gently. I let the hot, steaming bubbles start to relax me. With a deep sigh of relief, I just exhaled and thought to myself, this shit feels real good! Just as I finished my blunt, I was feeling real good and horny. I slipped two fingers down and parted my lips and began rubbing my clit. Just as I was singing out loud, the phone rings. Fuck that! I was enjoying myself. I let the answering machine get it. I was in my glory until I heard Jai's loud ass mouth, screaming through the damn phone.

*"Bitch, I know you there! Pick up the phone!"*

I just laughed out loud, and took my time getting out. It was time anyway. I quickly snatched the phone up and yelled through the phone. "What the fuck you want? Can't a bitch come home and chill the fuck out!? DAMN!"

"Oh bitch please! You wasn't doing shit anyway but smoking and probably playing with yourself." Damn, you know it's bad when my girls know I'm playing with myself! I kept it pushing like I didn't hear her. "Hahaha, whatever bitch, what's up?" I said as I walked over to the bed twisting my hair. She kept talking like what she said wasn't throwing shade. She continued to say, "Did you talk to Mia?"

"No, not yet, but she left me a message. I haven't called her back why?" I said.

Jai sounded very excited and said, "You remember Tone from 7th Ave.?"

Rolling my eyes, cause I never remembered people from back in the day, I quickly respond so she can get to the point. "Nah, not really." I said.

"Damn! You don't remember no fucking body, wit yo boogie ass!"

I'm irritated now, so I replied through gritted teeth, "Whatever, bitch! What about him?"

She insisted I knew this dude and started trying to refresh my memory. "You remember we use to go to those house parties? In the rec room? Mia use to always be like, that's her brother Tone. The one who was throwing parties and shit?"

Shaking my head, cause I really don't remember dude. I ain't say shit, just listened to her ass ramble.

"Remember when Fu got shot down there?" She said.

I answered quick as hell because I knew Fu. He used to rock with Big Daddy.

"Hell yeah! With his fine ass! That was one fine nigga." I said.

I started picturing his ass in my mind and thought to myself, I should have gave that nigga some. Jai's ass still talking while I'm in deep thought. "Well, Fu is Tone's brother. After that nigga got killed, he said fuck that shit! Now he got a business partner and they went legit. Anyhoo, Mia got some VIP passes to that new club downtown. I think the name of the club is "The Strip" or some shit. You wanna go?" Sitting with my towel wrapped around me, I'm feeling really relaxed. I said, "I don't know girl, I'm kinda tired. I don't really feel like being bothered with all them tired ass brothers tryna get some ass because they brought me a nine-dollar drink."

"Bitch please! You need some dick and I mean some new dick, not fat ass Big Daddy!"

"Oh girl, he called me tonight and left a message, but I deleted it. I'm not tryna go on a treasure hunt to find small jewels!" I was laughing so hard I was crying.

Maybe she's right; I should go. I might just find someone to break me off. Shit! I'm not looking for Mr. Right. I'm looking for Mr. Right now! Rolling my eyes, I said, "Alright, what time should I be ready? And whose car we taking? Better yet, I'm driving my own car.

You ride with Mia or drive your own car.  I might dip off with a handsome, big dick nigga and get this kitty wet!" I started looking in the mirror pouting my lips. With her sarcastic ass mouth she said, "Excuse the fuck outta me! Never mind my transportation. Jjust meet us outside The Strip around 11. By then, all the men, - the fine ones anyway, should be coming in."

"Now Jai, you and I both know, that all the cheap brothers are there before 10 just so they can get in for free. Any brother with a little paper coming late to be seen."

Jai tried to talk and laugh at the same time. She said, "Hell yeah! And Jai don't do cheap. I need a man who ain't gotta ask me for shat!"

"I feel you, but all I need is a nice long stroke by a man with a big dick, I'll see you later."

Later that night, I stepped back and looked in the mirror and said to myself,

*"Damn I look good."* I had on my black lace, damn near see through, Vera Wang, come fuck me dress. Along

with the red, fuck me, Gucci shoes. My chocolate is skin shining. My hair on fleek and I smell good! If I don't

get any tonight, then something gotta be wrong with them or they're gay! I reached the club and swayed my ass

towards Mia, and before I could even get close enough, she started yelling my name like she ain't seen me in

years.

"Hey, Topaz!" Mia said. Mia always said she liked calling me by my last name. She said it was more fitting.

She continued to say "I'm surprised to see you here. You know how you do on a Friday night. You'll smoke an

L and take it down."

Greeting her with a kiss, I said, "Yeah well I got my L in the car and hopefully someone will take me down." I

said. Mia was dressed casual and fly. She looked as if she didn't have to try. She's just gorgeous. She had on a

pair of True jeans that was tight as hell and it made her booty pop. She was killing it with those black strappy

shoes. The heels were about 6 inches high. She loved her shoes and her shoe game is tight as hell. I gotta

remind myself to borrow those bad boys right there! She was rocking this black, plunging neck blouse that

showed her tattoo. After looking at her up and down I said, "Damn girl, you killin it tonight!"

Poking her booty out and giving me duck lips. She said, "You know how we do! I ain't the only one killing it.

Looks like you tryna get some tonight." Mia giggled and gave me a high five. Jai pulled up and caught the end

of the conversation. With her loud ass voice she said,

"I know that's right. Now let's go and make all the women hate us and all the men want us."

Jai so crazy and she knows she hot shit tonight. She had on a red pantsuit that was sexy

and conservative. She was killing it too! When she took her jacket off, the top looked like someone was

slashing her ass. It's so fierce and it showed all of her tatas. We walked in and all eyes were on us. The women

were hating too! They were whispering and shit, but it's cool, because we know why they hate! The music was

right. Dj Snaxx was spinning the club classic, *Just Us*. The club was rocking and of course we couldn't find a good spot that we wanted to be in. There were no tables left. The gentlemen sitting offered us their table. The waiter came over and took our drink order. When he returned he said, "The gentleman at the bar bought your first round." We turned and looked, and he nodded. Jai was cheesing and shit! I looked at her and said, "Damn Jai! It's just a drink be easy. I bet the man can count how many teeth in your mouth."

"Hell, I'm just being friendly and besides he's cute."

I just sucked my teeth and said, "Jai, he's not my type, so go for it girl."

She didn't even look at me when just kept staring at the man and said, "Topaz, do you really have a type tonight?"

"Fuck you, Jai!" I said, as I reached for my margarita. Mia grabbed her bag and got up. I looked at her up and down. "Where you going?" I asked. She took a sip of her drink, and started to walk away and said, "I see some of my peoples, I'll be back."

Mia's always running into her peoples. Jai is just sitting there rocking back and forth to the music. Jai got up and said, "Erica, I'll be back, I'm going over to say thank you to Mr. Cutie for buying our drinks." When she said that, I started looking for my purse like it was lost. I yelled loud enough for her to hear me over the music. "Damn! Why every time we go out, y'all always end up leaving me alone at the damn able!? Well, not tonight honey; I'm going over to the bar. Shit! I look too good not to be seen."

"I know that's right girl, work that shit!" Jai said.

So I got up and swayed myself over to the bar. I could feel all eyes on me. I really started working it. Making the women hot and the men too, for that matter! As I sat at the bar, I seen this fine nigga approaching Mia, grinning with them bright white teeth. I'm tryna read his lips. I overheard them talking.

"Mia, what's up? How are you?" He said.

"Hey Tone, what's up? I see the club is packed! Congratulations on your grand opening."

He kissed Mia on the cheek and said, "Thanks babe, so what's up? You looking fine as usual. I know you didn't come by yourself, where your peoples?" Mia started blushing hard as hell. Something more is going on with them cause she smiling too hard.

"Oh, now you know I got my girls up in here," she replied. I couldn't hear shit else because this fine chocolate brother was walking towards them. All I can think about is his lips. The brother is fine! I moved in a little closer because I needed to hear his voice.

"Hey Tone, let me holla at you for a minute," he said.

Just like I thought, he sounded sexy as hell. That voice matched his sexiness. Tone grabbed Mia's hand.

"Excuse me Mia, this is Jahmar Morton, my business partner. Jah, this is Mia, she's like my little sister. So no funny ideas."

He stretched his hand out to shake it but, Mia just gave him her fingertips, like she didn't really wanna shake it.

"Hey Mia, how you doing?" Sexy chocolate said.

"I'm good, how are you?" She said.

"Yes, you are baby!" He was licking his juicy lips. I almost started drooling.

Tone pulled Jah's arm. "Hey hey now, didn't I say no funny ideas!?"

"Just playing playa, but I really do need to talk to you, in private." Tone looked around and glanced at me. He nodded with a smile like he recognized me. He then grabbed Mia's arm and said, "Mia, you and your girls get drinks on the house. I'll be back."

"Ok, cool," she said.

As she was walking away, I heard Mr. Jahmar say, "Yo, a brother can't be giving away drinks and shit. How the fuck we supposed to make money, if you giving away shit!?" He put a cigar in his mouth, like it was lit. Tone was looking around the club like he was enjoying the vibe. He cut his eyes at Jah and said, "Chill out, Jah! Mia is family and anything she wants and need, she got that! She has gotten me outta some real shit a few times. She may look fine as wine, and believe

me she is, but she can be a real ride and die chick if need be."

I just laughed thinking to myself, Tone talk like he got a thang for Mia. It's more than friendship. I acted like I ain't hear that whole convo. I refocused on the men while I sipped on my drink. I started feeling a little irritated that Jai and Mia always leaving me alone. It's cool though, because Ms. Topaz gone get her some tonight, believe that one. The men are loving me tonight. I've had tall ones, short ones, fat ones, and stank ones, and ones with way too much damn cologne on, buying me drinks. No one turned me on in the slightest way. This is such bullshit! I should've stayed my ass at home. I'm gonna go sit in my car and smoke this L. Maybe some of these brothers will start to look good to me. Damn! This shit is packed wall to wall. I can barely get through. The whole time I was saying, "Excuse me, excuse me, excuse me." Damn! Finally, in the fresh air. All I smelled is perfume and cigarettes and it stunk.  Especially mixed with stale cigars and alcohol. The men were alright, just no Mr. Right now. I couldn't wait to sit in the car.

Once I got in, I reached for my L that's been waiting for me in the ashtray. I lit it and took a few pulls before realizing I didn't wanna smell like weed. So I stood outside the car and smoked.  At least I have the night air blowing through. As I stood there, I saw some really fine potentials. I mean fine brothers coming and going. Shiiid, I'm trying to see one of them fine asses. Where the hell they asses at? I damn sure didn't see anybody that looked like them in there. It must be a secret room in there somewhere. Where the hell is Mia? She is supposed to have the hook up! While standing there in thought, my blunt went out and so Isaid, fuck it! I got a good buzz. I placed the blunt back in the ashtray and sprayed on some perfume.

I don't want to stink of weed. Just as I was about to close the door, I saw that fine dark brother that Tone and Mia was talking to earlier. Damn! He looking fine as he wanna look. He stands about 5'10",with big brown eyes, and these little twists in his hair. Damn! I'd fuck him! Finally, I spot one! So I slammed my car door real hard to get his attention, and the shit worked! He turned around and  looked at me from head to toe. He said,"Damn ma, you gonna break that door, closing it like that."

Looking down at the door handle like, it really just slipped.  "Yeah I know, I didn't mean to do that, but the handle slipped." I said.

"How's the club? Is it packed?" He asked, as he walked towards me with that Denzel swag. "Yeah, the club is lit. The music is rocking and the drinks are nice for the price."

He leaned on my car and said,  "So, where's your date? Or did you come alone?"

"No, I didn't bring a date. Where's your date?" I said. He grabbed my hand and pulled me real gentle.  "No! So let me escort you inside and buy you a drink." Wait, he said no, so then he's not alone? Oh hell! Fuck it. When we walked into the club, he didn't get the normal pat down. He took me straight to the back of the club. There were like 5 or 6 doors marked VIP. He took me to VIP #5. As soon as the door closed behind us, I sat down. It was like he flipped a switch, because next thing I know, the door opens and the waitress walks in with a bottle and two glasses! He tipped her lovely and she left. He poured me a drink and handed it to me.

"Thank you, Mr. umm?" Shit what the fuck is his name? He knew I didn't know his name. He quickly responded, "Jahmar, Jahmar Morton."

"Thank you, Mr. Jahmar Morton."

He pulled out a chair for me to sit. He tryna remember my name, but I never told him. He stumbles with his words and says. "You're welcome Ms….."

"Topaz, just Topaz." I said.

"Oh ok, Ms. Topaz, I like that name! A rare gem! Let me find out I hit the gold mine! So did you enjoy your blunt?"

"Yes I did, why you ask?"

He walked over to this table that had a single drawer. He pulled out a fat ass bag and a blunt.

"I was wondering because I have my own stash, and I don't wanna smoke alone. So, what's up?"

Oh, hell no, something not right. I'm not Mary from the Country Club. My inner hoodrat self is telling me something a little off. Shit, for all I know, that weed could be laced with some other shit. And how the fuck he know I was outside smoking? I just said, "No thank you, I'm good. I have to drive home, I'll just watch you smoke." To keep him from asking me anymore questions, I figured I'd start my own q & a. "So, Mr. Morton, what do you do for a living?"

This mofo sexy as hell and he knows it too. The way he looked after he took a pull of that blunt. The way the smoke swept past his face, damn! In his sexy voice, he said, "I'm co-owner of this club."

Crossing my legs, I sat back in the chair. I said, "That's good, so you know my sister Mia? She said she knew the owner."

"No, I don't know a Mia," licking his lips before he continued, "maybe she know my partner, Tone."

"Is this your only club?" I asked. I only asked because I'm tryna see where his paper at.

"Yes it is, but I plan on doing a lot of new things. I wanna own a couple of clothing stores and invest in some kind of restaurant."

Tryna sound enthusiastic I said, "oh ok, that's what's up."

He seemed real cool and smart. He has goals and ambition. We talked for hours and I learned that he's from 18th Ave. Him and Tone are best friends and he use to hustle hard. They were hugging the block heavy. One night him, Tone and Tone's brother, Fu, were out getting something to eat and as they were leaving the chicken shack on Elizabeth Ave., some niggas came through and started bussing. Fuwas shot and was killed. As he was talking, I'm thinking, this nigga probably still hustling. I continued to listen.

"After my homie was killed, I decided to turn my dirty money into legit money," he said.

As much as I loved his voice. I was getting sleepy so, I decided to excuse myself. "Well Jahmar," searching for my car keys. Tryna not look him in those eyes of his.

He said, "Please, call me Jah."

"Ok Jah, it's been nice chilling with you." I said.

He got up to walk me out and he said, "I enjoyed your company as well, Ms. Topaz."

I was looking for something nice to say, I just responded, "Your club is really hot. Maybe we'll see each other again. Soon." As I stood up, I wanted him to throw me on the that little ass table and just fuck the shit outta me. I know that's not happening; well at least not tonight. He reached inside his desk and gave me his card.

"Ms. Topaz, call me sometime and maybe we'll hook up and burn some trees or something."

As I took his card, he grabbed my wrist and pulled me close and kissed me on my forehead! Damn! That was the sexiest kiss I got in a long time. I gotta make it my business to see him again! To my surprise, when I got outside, the sun was coming up. I didn't know it was so late, or early I should say. I exited through a back door, so I didn't even realize the club was closed. The music was still playing though. As I got into my car, I spotted my half of blunt. I turned my cd on, with my diva, Mary J Blige, playing and toked on my weed. Chilling on my ride home. Next thing I know, my cell phone rings. I hate when I'm grooving and shit; singing at the top of my lungs and I get interrupted! I answered with urgency.

"Hello, this is Topaz."

"Oh, bitch please, where you at?" Mia said.

"Good morning to you too, Mia. I'm on my way home. What's up?"

"Home? Home from where? Oh shit, bitch! You got you some dick last night?" She said.

"No, but I got a real good prospect. I'm just leaving The Strip."

Mia has this way of making this screeching loud ass noise when she's excited. Right away she started

questioning me. "What you mean, you just leaving the club? The club closed at 3am. It's fucking 6:30. I

thought you'd be on your way to the gym. Sooo, who the fuck were you with at the club?"

"Damn, Mia! To make a long story short, I was with Jah."

"Who the hell is Jah? Oh wait, he co-owns the club. You talking about Jahmar Morton?"

"Damn! Who don't you know? How you know him Mia?" I asked her.

"I met him last night, Tone introduced us," she said.

Awe damn, there goes my prospect! I knew she didn't really know him. My ass was being nosy last night when

she got the introduction. Mia sucked her teeth like a true Jamaican. She said, "That brother fine as hell, Topaz!"

"Yeah, I know." I said. I hope he and Mia don't hook up. Imma be mad, not at Mia, but at

him! He made it seem like, he was really feeling me. I didn't forget how he flirted with Mia. Let me find out he

fishing and tryna see who bite first. Out of curiosity I asked her, "So Mia, what's up? Should I fall back or nah?"

"Oh no girl, do you! It's not like that at all. He was too busy tryna talk to Tone, rather than trying to get with

me."

Yes! I'm glad that what I was thinking was not the case. I wanna fuck his fine ass, and I'mma

fuck him real good. I'm rushing Mia off the phone because, I'm tryna get my groove back.

"Ok girl, let me get off this phone. You fucked up my groove and shit. I gotta run to my house

and change; grab my gym bag and head to the gym. Saturdays get packed real quick. I'll holla at

you later, maybe we can go to the mall or do lunch."

****

I met Mia at Momma L kitchen to have lunch. I walked in to see my two besties Mia and Jai, waiting on me. I started walking towards them grinning, tryna walk like America's Next Top Model. "Well, hello ladies!" I said. Mia spoke first and loud. "Hey, Topaz."

Giving air kisses I said, "Hey, Mia. What's up?" I pulled out the chair sitting closer to Jai. I saw Jai giving me the side eye. I looked at her and said, "Jai, I meant to call you, but I was busy today and I needed a fucking nap. I totally forgot to call you to meet us for lunch. I was sure that Mia, the event planner, would call you." As soon as I sat down, the waiter brought over three glasses of wine and took our orders. Checking my phone to see if Jah called, I looked up and said, "So, what's up with y'all today?"

Jai ain't waste no time to start grilling me about last night. She gulped her wine like she needed it."Oh! Don't even try it, Erica. What's up with you and this dude, Jahmar? Mia told me you were chilling at the club. ….. Until 6:30 this morning, boo! So, spill the tea."

I sipped my wine and cleared my throat, like I had some good tea to spill. "Well, if you must know, he cool peoples. He took me to the VIP Room. Where he smoked and I had a drink or two."

"Hold up, Topaz, what you mean he smoked?" Mia said.

Feeling like a fiend I said, "Damn, Mia! I mean he smoked and I didn't. Is it really that hard for you to believe?"

In unison they said, "Yeah."

I rolled my eyes as hard as I could and smartly said, "Anyway, I was drinking and I needed to be on point. I would have fucked him last night and I didn't want it to seem like, I'm some kinda hoe. Those days are over!"

Jai always gotta be the one to remind me of some shit. She started laughing and said, "But Erica, didn't you say last night that, all you wanted was to find a man and fuck him?" Jai think she cute. Acting like she sipping tea from her wine glass.

"Yes, I did say that Jai, but I do wanna know something about him." I said.

As we sat there eating our catfish and wild rice, we talked about last night and what we were doing later on that evening. I planned on meeting Jah tonight for dinner at Savoy's lounge and restaurant. Mia and Jai are going back to The Strip to get their party on.

**** 

*"I'm so fly,"* I told myself, as I pranced around in the mirror. Jah said he wanted to go out for dinner. We've been out three times this week and it's cool and all, but I wanna fuck. I don't wanna be wined and dined but, fuck it. I guess he can spend a little change. He said he'll call when he's close to the house. I bet he looks good as usual. The other night when he came to pick me up, he had on this pink and white button up shirt, with French cuffs, and some serious bling. A pair of white slacks and some nice ass shoes. He looked so good that, as soon as I opened the door to let him in, my fucking panties got soaking wet! I hope he plans on fucking me tonight, because I got my 'fuck me' panties on. My phone starts ringing, this must be him.

"Hello." I answered in my sexy voice.

"Oh please, who you thought I was?"

I rolled my eyes with the look of being bothered, because it was Jai's ass. "What's up, Jai?" I said.

"Hey girl, you must have thought I was Jah, you tryna sound all sexy and shit."

"Whatever, I always answer the phone like that. So, what's up? I'm about to go out, so make it quick."

Jai's always tryna figure shit out, she quickly responded. "Damn, y'all always going out. What's this date number 6 or 7? That's your man now?"

"Man? Hell no! I'm just tryna get some, but we cool though. We'll be more cool once he give me some of that

D!" I heard a beep, it was my other line.

"Jai, I gotta go, that's my other end; I'll talk to you tomorrow and tell Mia she better be cooking

Sunday dinner tomorrow!"

CLICK!

Hello," I said, tryna sound sexy.

"Hey Topaz, I'm outside. Do you want me to come in?" Jah's deep voice gave me goose bumps.

"Come in, I'm almost ready." I said.

As soon as I hung up, I ran to look at myself once again, just to make sure that I'm straight; and I was. I just

needed a little lip gloss, a little oil sheen for my hair, and put my shoes on. He can wait downstairs while I do

that. When I opened the door, the brother was looking good, but I didn't expect anything less.  He had on some

khaki pants, with a beige polo shirt, and some crispy, fresh Timbs. Never seen him dressed down before and he

was still fine. He doesn't look hood at all. I was looking good too, with my tight ass jeans and my Donna Karan

shirt, and them bad ass shoes that I borrowed from Mia. Shit, we look too good to leave the house. I promise

you this, he will be giving me some tonight. We went to this very laid back soul food restaurant in the hood and

baby, we was in the hood HOOD!  I loved the atmosphere though. It looked like my Nana and'em was at home

cooking, while I chilled out with my boyfriend on the couch, listening to Soft Jazz. It was a really nice surprise.

Dinner was good and we talked a lot this time. I guess because we smoked on the way to the restaurant, Jahmar

was really talking, he started talking about his past and his past criminal activities. He must have forgotten, he

told me about his boy Fu getting shot, because he told me again. I can tell that the incident scared the shit outta

him. He really wants to go legit, however the people he still says are his brothers, are still hustlers and I'm far

from stupid. This brother was and still is, a big time drug dealer and is

doing big things. After a few shots, he really started talking . Just like I thought, this nigga

started talking about business again. Now he says he's still in the game but, not like he use to

be. He invested his money in the night club and plans to open up a few more businesses.

I'm no fool and I'm from the hood and niggas in the game usually stay in the game. There is only one way out and that's death. Shit, you can even hustle in prison. He thinks he

slick, but he into the game more than he saying, but I don't give a fuck. I'm just looking for a

good fuck and that's why I gotta stop chilling with him. He might really start feeling me and I'm not looking for

a commitment right now. If I was into hustlers, full time or part time, he wouldn't be the one. Instant turn off!

I'm ready to go.

# Me'asha Lawson

# (Mia)

Shit, a sista tired. I just wrapped up my last banquet for the week. As tired as I am, I'm going to

a party tonight at the club with Jai. I don't know what's up with Topaz, a sista been working

hard all week, let me call her....

**(phone ringing)**

She answered and I said, "Hey Tee, what's up?"

Sounding like she was busy, she quickly answered and said, "Hey Mia, nothing I'm almost done with work. It's

been a hectic week. Especially since we go to press next week. Other than that, I'm cool. What's up with you?"

"Nothing much, about to light this blunt. I just got done doing a banquet for 350 people. It was a birthday party

for an 85-year-old woman. I'm tired as hell, but a bitch still going out to turn up and shake my ass. Jai and I are

going, so what time will you be ready?"

"Bitch please! I wish, I got too much work to do. You know I ain't gonna be right until my magazine comes out

and I get them numbers! So it's a wrap for me, for at least 2 weeks!"

I just kept it moving because I knew she would say that. "Alright girl, now don't say you didn't know about us

going out later. I'll tell your boo what's up for you." I said.

"My boo? And who might that be?" Topaz said.

I laughed at the question and said, "Now girl, you know that Jah is going to be your new boo!"

"No, the fuck he not! I hadn't even spoke to Jah. The last time we talked, he was telling me too much of his personal shit. Wanting to wine and dine me and shit. A brother trying to hook a sista, wife me up, and shit. Fuck all that! All I wanted was the dick and not all that extra bullshit.  Besides that, I know the nigga still hugging the streets and I just can't deal with that!"

"I feel you, but you should fuck him anyway. The brother fine as hell." I said.

"Now girl, you know my shit is the bomb and the way this brother acting, he'll fuck around and fall in love with a bitch. Nope not this one!" She said.

I had to get off the phone with her ass. I said, "Bitch you crazy and I gotta go. I'll talk to you soon."


CLICK!


Oh well, more drinks for me. I gotta put my fly shit on tonight because the last time I was there, the ballers were out and about. I gotta make sure that they don't know my peoples, because my peoples will be watching me. Just as I was getting out the shower, my phone started ringing.

I bet this is Jai, checking to see how far I am on getting dressed. I picked up the phone and quickly answered.

"20 minutes, Jai! Damn, you be on it."

"Hey, lady."  He said, with that sultry voice. I was surprised to hear his voice, but not really.

"Hey you, what's up? I thought you were Jai." I said.

"I see and are you disappointed?"

"Not at all, I'm actually happy to hear your voice."

He didn't respond to that, but he tried to sound sweet. He calmly said, "So, what you and Jai got planned that you need 20 minutes?"

"We going to the club." I said

"Damn momma, why you always gotta be at the club shaking your ass?"

I love it when he calls me momma. Sometimes he calls me sweet momma. I try to sound sweet as possible when

I replied. "Be easy baby, I only go to have a good time and to chill with my girls."

"Yeah right, every time I come in the club it be some nigga in your face!" He said

"Yeah, but I don't pay them no mind. I'm with you and I always let a brother know that I'm spoken for."

He sounded mad now. "I bet if those niggas knew who I was, they wouldn't fuck with you on that level."

Oh boy, here we go again! Trying to convince him, I said as sweet as possible, "Baby, listen, I promise you in

due time everyone will know about you and us."

He took a long pause and I knew that the whole, "*I'm tired*" convo was about to happen.

"Lil momma, I'm tired of having to sneak around and shit. We gotta go out of town just to spend a little time

together out in the open."

"I'm tired of the shit, too. It'll be over real soon." I said.

"One more question Mia, why haven't you told your girls about me or us?"

"Babe, until you go fully legit, I can't say anything. If people knew you were my man, it may hurt my

businesses. I think we should wait until all this court shit is over and your name not as tarnished. Forthe record,

my girls know of you just not who you are." I'm tired of talking about this shit. I'm tired of sparing everybody

else's feelings. It's about to be all about me! My silence must have let him know.

"Ok momma, I'm done talking about it and I'll do what you ask of me. I'mma chill out, but one day soon

dammit, you gonna be showing my fine ass off!"

"Thanks babe, I gotta go and I'll see you later. You are going to club tonight?"

"Of course, because you'll be there and I gotta watch you and them niggas," he said.

Rolling my eyes again, but deep inside, I love how he wants to protect me. "Baby, I don't need watching. You

can trust me. I'll see you later ok?" I said.

"Alright, I'll see you later," he said.

Damn, I knew that nigga couldn't be at the club without watching me all night. The crazy part is, I don't be

doing shit. I just be chilling with my peoples and talking shit. Hell, even if he wasn't at the club, I still wouldn't

be doing shit! But it's my fault he doubting me and us. Because he knows I have a man in LA. I don't have much time now.  I better hurry up.  Jai will have a fit if we not there early enough to get a good parking spot close to the doors. Allbecause her ass don't wanna walk too far, with them 6 inch heels. Tryna be sexy and shit!

# "GIRL TALK"

# Mia

"Topaz, this is Mia, me and Jai are in the car and we are on our way over there. So. get the fuck up or if you are up, put down the blunt, and turn the vibrator off, and open the door."

Jai turned and looked at me and said, "What she say, Mia?"

I put my phone back on the charger and laughed. "Nothing, that was her answering machine." I said. "Now you know, she's there and she probably still working. Which means she's gonna be a straight bitch. We both know how she is around this time of the month. It's like she has p.m.s twice a month. Once for her period and again when the issue of her magazine comes out."

Tryna find my Gucci cd, I said, "Yeah, but I don't give a fuck! Everyone needs a break sometimes and we gonna give her one."

# Topaz

BANG BANG BANG!! BELL RINGING...

Taking my gat damn time, and peeking out the window like I don't want them to see me, but I

really want them to see me. Jai started looking in the peek hole. So I said, "Y'all some rude bitches, just

showing up at a bitch house, without being announced or invited and shit."

Mia and her big mouth always got something to say. I stood there trying to block the

door and Mia said, "Whatever, I left you a message. You should've checked your voicemail and you would've

known, me & Jai were on our way!"

I cracked the door just a little, and they just pushed the door right past my ass. Right away Mia just started to

talk, like they didn't just show up unannounced and she was talking shit too. Mia said, "Jai picked up some

fresh weed, straight off the top, and two six packs of Bahama mama wine coolers and I brought food."

She started pulling all these tin pans out the greasy brown bags and she ain't skipping a beat. Not once did she

take a breath, she continued and said, "I picked up some of that grilled chicken and Spanish rice, that you and

Jai love so much. I do not plan on cooking today or the next few days."

I closed the door and did one of those, curtsy things that people do when greeting Royal people.

"Being the gracious host that I am, welcome ladies and please make yourself at home. I actually get away with doing nothing today. Hey Mia, grab some plates while you're in the kitchen."

I started cleaning up and shit, tryna make room for us to eat. "Let me make room and move all my work mess!" I started moving my laptop off the couch and removed all the papers that were laying across the table. I looked up and saw Jai standing there with her hands on her hips talking about, "Oh NOOOW, you wanna throw the welcome mat down, because we got goodies."

"Whatever Jai, I'm surprised to see your ass ain't at the club tonight. You and Mia love that club."

Jai sat down and started putting the bags on the table. She pulled out the wine coolers and a blunt wrap and said, "Humph, I can remember somebody else loving the club too."

I rolled my eyes at Jai and looked in the kitchen at Mia with the death stare, because Mia always gotta put her 2 cents in and in true Mia form, she starts yelling from the kitchen and said, "No Jai, it wasn't the club she was loving, more like loving the club owner!"

"Damn, Mia! You all the way in the kitchen and in here too!"

"Topaz, you know I speak truth!"

"Hahaha, forget both of y'all bitches."

I snatched the blunt from Jai and said, "Jai give me that blunt, before you fuck it up."

Jai handed me the blunt fast as hell, like she was waiting for me to say something about it. She can't roll a good blunt to save her life.

Opening one of those Bahama's Jai said, "Erica, you should've came out with us. We had so much fun. Mia was the life of the party, as usual."

Mia walked in with plates and sat down next to me and bragging. "I can't help it. I know a lot of people and my business lets me come across a lot of people, too. Plus, I have different connections and people know, I'm the person to come to for any and everything. I AM THE DAMN CONNECT!"

Jaii was shoving food in her mouth, but managed to say, "Yes, you are queen connect and I'm glad that one of those connects, was Tone and Jah. Shiiid last night them brothers was hooking us up on the drinks. Even threw in a couple of bottles of Moet. That's some nasty ass shit, but I bet my ass drank that shit though!"

Mia licked her fingers. "Tone my peoples, he's like my brother, but y'all know that already. Ever since I did that bday party for his momma for damn near free, he's been hooking me up and anybody I bring with me. I guess that's his way of repaying me." I don't know about this Tone, I mean yeah, he's cool, but he's into some crazy bullshit. When we were younger this nigga stole 10 grand from this big time dealer, and instead of killing Tone, he made him work for him and he been dirty ever since. I don't want Mia getting caught in a crossfire with any of his bullshit. Whelp moving on, I quickly changed the subject. I didn't want it to seem like I don't like Tone. I asked Jai a question instead. "So Jai, you've been going to the club every weekend since it

opened, what's up with the men? I know they be stalking ya ass!"

"Well, up until last night I really haven't been feeling them brothers. Last night I met this fine ass brother named Kaseem. He is sexy as hell! He's brown skin, about 6'2" tall, and he has the prettiest white teeth, I have ever seen. Built like Jaheim, but sexier. I'll see what he's all about come next week, cause we do have a date. Owwww!"

Here go Mia and that big mouth again. "Ok now Jai, get that shit!"

"Shut up, Mia! Always talking about get that shit, and just what you getting?" I said.

Mia snapped that head around and said, "I'm getting dick and so will Jai in about a week. Question is, what the fuck you getting, Topaz?"

Before I got a chance to let Mia know what I'm getting Jai says, "Topaz, I've been meaning to ask you, why you stop fucking with Jah?"

"Damn, I thought Mia told you why." I said.

Shaking her head, she said, "You know she don't remember shit! She almost forgot

to pick me up today!" Mia responded real quickly. She put the chicken down and she tried to sound serious. "Now Jai, you know ya ass is lying, I did not!"

Scooping up her rice and right before she ate it, Jai said, "Whatever! Yes, you did."

I can only laugh at these two. "Y'all so crazy."

Jai just gotta prove her point. She continued to say, "For real Erica, if I didn't call Mia to ask about the damn

weed, she would have forgotten all about me and she was already on her way when I called her ass."

Mia choked off that weed I passed her and said, "Jai that's not true, I was just leaving

my people's house when you called me."

With her mouth twisted Jai said, "Yeah ok, when I asked you where you were, you said on your way to Topaz

house, I said oh without me? Then you laughed and said, 'oh shit! Come outside, I'll be there in five minutes."

Mia couldn't help but laugh because she knew what Jai was saying was true. The only thing she could say was,

"That didn't mean that I forgot about you. I was just a little distracted."

Jai pushed her lips up in a pout and said, "Yeah I bet, anyway Erica what happened?"

"Nothing really happened, Jai. He's just looking for something that I'm not willing to give right

now."

Mia always gotta be the one to say some slick shit. As she picked at that chicken, she said,

"What that nigga want, a fucking kidney or some shit?"

Shaking my head, I simply said, "Nah Mia, he wants a wife, and I don't want that right now. I can't handle my

new position and a man, too. You know they need a lot of attention and I don't have time for all that. All I

wanted was some good ass sex. Mia, you know my shit will have a nigga sprung."

Laughing hard as hell Mia replied, "Hell yeah, that's why you can't get rid of big ass, Big Daddy."

I smirked because she's right. I paused before continuing to say, "Besides that, Jah is still in the street game

and those days are over for me."

Mia started clearing her throat. "Excuse me, Ms. Topaz, but isn't Big Daddy a hustler?"

There Mia go again, always pointing out the obvious. I put my feet under me and got real comfortable, cause

I'm high and I said, "Yeah, but he ain't my man and when his ass get locked up, I'm not the one who bails him

out and I don't do collect calls."

Mia interrupted my convo and saying, "I was talking to Tone the other night and he said that,

Jahmar is caking. He also said that Jah is about to open a restaurant and lounge. The brother got

serious money."

I had to remind Mia what kind of money, I said, "Yeah Mia, drug money! And when did you have this conversation with Tone?"

She started pulling her hair back into a bun and said, "The other night, why?"

Jai quickly said, what I was thinking. "Oh Mia, let me find out, you fucking Tone." Jai said.

Mia cocked her head to the side and said, "Now Jai, you know that Jayson is my one and only true love. Tone is just my peoples and we like family."

Now I'm fucking with her, the way she been fucking with me all night and I said, "So what we're y'all talking about, other than me and Jah?" Mia sounded a little annoyed now and said, "Truth be told, Ms. Topaz, who thinks that everything is about her. We were talking about Jah and his restaurant and me doing business with them. They need a head chef. I just brought you up, to see if I could get any inside information on what Jah is saying about you."

I'm curious now so, I asked, "And?"

She tried to be funny, like she not comprehending the question and said, "And what?"

I'm blinking fast, like I'm sending signals and asked, "Did you get any info, inspector fucking gadget?" Mia being funny now with her response and says, "Maybe and what difference does it make? You said you wasn't fucking with him!"

I'm feeling annoyed now so I tell her, "I'm not. I'm just interested in what he thinks!" As usual, here comes Jai co-signing shit and says, "Mia? Is it me, or did Erica say a few months ago,

that she wanted a man and a family?"

Nodding her head in agreement, Mia said, "I do recall that statement, Jai. So Topaz, what's changed?"

I grabbed a bottle and said, "Nothing's changed, I just need a man who has ambition. A man who has goals and wants shit out of life. Not no part time hustler and part time business man."

Jai is always so trustworthy, she's always playing help woman and thinks everybody can change. Here she go defending his ass. "Yeah ok, but he has goals and ambition. He owns one club and about to own a restaurant. Maybe he does want something out of life. Which is why he's turning that drug money, into legit money."

Tired of talking about it, I simply said, "Well ok, when and if he ever goes legit, I might give the brother another chance."

Jai just gotta have the last word. "I hope nobody else snatches his ass up, or you'll be assed out."

Taking the heat off my ass, I put Mia back in the hot seat and asked her a serious question.

"Mia, have you ever thought about the role you would play, if you went into business with

those two hustlers?" I said.

"My role? Shit, I don't play a role. As far as I'm concerned, I am the chef! My role is cooking food three nights

a week."

Jai sounded just as concerned as I was when she said, "What if something happens and the feds wanna know,

what you know? You can't afford to have your name mixed up in any bullshit."

I agreed and said, "Mia, you know Jai is right. How you gonna have your business linked to a place built with

drug money? If Jah got so much money, I'm quite sure the feds or the police know Mr. Morton and his financial

background. You don't want that type of attention drawn to your name, or your business."

She sounds like her mind is made up. She simply stated, "Tone said that the new business was paid for with

legit money; Anyway Tone would never put me in any type of illegal shit. When his brother Fu got shot, that

was his turning point. I guess he said fuck it, without his partner he ain't doing it no more. I believe him when

he says, he's done."

Jai and I looked at each other and before I could say anything Jai said, "Damn! Sounds like you and Tone is

pretty tight, huh?"

"Jai, why is it that you always think men and women can't be friends without fucking? You and Jayson are real

tight too, and y'all call each other brother and sister."

My girl Jai quickly points out the obvious fact and says, "Yeah, but the difference is me and Jay been friends

since 6th grade. We grew up together, we from the same hood and we've been friends for over 25 years. You've

known Tone for what 3 years? That's not long at all. Shit the way you talk about him, seem like y'all fucking."

"Now Jai, please! I'm not fucking Tone. If I was you and Topaz would know."

Jai chuckled and said, "How?"

Mia answered quickly and said, "I would tell you Jai, that's how!"

Jai continued to say, "All I'm saying is, you and Tone suspect."

Mia feeling the need to explain herself continues to say, "I've known Tone since we were kids, too. You seem to have selective memory. We use to hang out with them at those house parties. Once he got caught up in the streets, we drifted apart and I went to college. When I came home one summer, I ran into him at the Chicken Shack and we been tight since then." She looked like she was reminiscing about an old lover. She was grinning hard and shit. I felt like putting my two cents in, just like she does and I said, "Don't worry Mia, I believe you. I know you in love with Jay, even though he's in LA and you're here." I paused for about five seconds and said, "With a wet kitty, and Tone is your type."

Mia laughed, but not really and said, "Hahaha Topaz, my kitty is just fine thank you! If I wanted or needed some dick, I'll take my ass to LA."

Acting surprised I said, "Oh! So that's what them business trips be about, huh?"

She laughed out loud and said, "Hell yeah Erica, it's not a lie, shiid it's handling my business!"

I'm grabbing my chest like old women do when hearing something shocking.

Jai starts acting too and said, "Oh well, excuse the fuck outta me Ms. Mia! We stand corrected."

Mia acting like it's nothing and says, "You excuse Ms. Jai, but next time worry about why yo ass ain'tgetting none."

Jai replied quietly and said, "I'm working on it."

We smoked about 3 blunts, fucked that food up, and talked shit all night! I love my sisters. Mia, Jai and I will forever be sisters.

# Jaiden Thomas

# Jai

I got my Mary playing and I'm looking good as I wanna look. I'm in a real good mood tonight,

and I'm feeling real good too. I drank three glasses of wine. Tryna relax before my date with

Kaseem Philips. This fine ass chocolate brother, I met at the Strip. He had me at hello! He fine as

hell, with no kids and no wife! Just a hard working marketing exec., I'm so excited about this. I'm prancing

around in my undies and shoes singing my heart out, to Mary's *Real Love*, like I'm the diva. It's almost 7:30 and

I need to put my clothes on and unwrap my hair. I hope this dude is not wasting my time and beauty tonight. I'm

putting on my black and sequin halter blouse, and my black gauchos with a silver belt, with my black stilettos. I

was sexy as hell! These shoes

make the arch in my back deeper; My butt bigger and my walk sexier than what it already is.

Kaseem needs to see, what he'll be missing, if he a bullshitter or what he'll get if he plays his cards right. I know

that I'm fine as hell, but I want him to know my inner beauty too.  My likes and my dislikes and even my crazy,

sometime ghetto fabulous ways. I like going out and flirting and meeting different types of brothers, but truth be told, I'm ready to settle down with one man. One who will love me unconditionally. One who will love me when I'm wrong. I want to be able to share my life and dreams with that one. I don't know if it's gonna be Kaseem, I'll have to see

what he's all about. Whelp, one last look in the mirror at my fine ass and then I'll sit in the living

room and wait for him to call.

# Kaseem Philips

"Kaseem, where you going?"

Looking confused I said, "Baby, I told you I have a dinner meeting to attend tonight and I'll be home around 10:30 or so." I love my wife Trina, but she has lost her appeal. I know that sounds mean, but it's true. All she wants to talk about is what the house needs and what she and the boys need and wants. What about me? Somewhere down the road she forgot about me and us. I just miss the time we use to share together, before the boys and the ring. She has changed drastically. I'll never leave my family though! I use the other women for sexual shit, or just when I wanna go out and party a little. I always ask Trina if she wanna do something without the boys and when she says no, I still go, just without her. Looking in the mirror, to make sure I'm straight, my son walks in and he says, "Daddy, where you going?" My son loves running and jumping into my arms! I picked him up and said, "Hey big man, I gotta go to work. I'll be back before you go to bed, be good for Mommy ok and remember, you the man till I get back."

I give him multiple kisses all over his face and put him down on the floor. My oldest son KJ (Kaseem Jr) is 13, and smart as hell, just like I was when I was his age. I make sure I guide him and his little brother, Nagee, who is 6, in the right direction. My son Nagee, looks just like my beautiful wife, with those big, brown, innocent eyes, and a smile, that will make you melt, just like my wife. When I first noticed my wife, it was that smile and those eyes that got me. I really do love my family. I wouldn't trade them in for nothing in this world. I go to kiss my wife and she moved. I didn't like that at all! I just looked at her and said, "Ok babe, I'm going and I'll see you guys when I get home."

"Kas, I love you."

I went in one more time for my kiss and this time, she didn't move and I said, "I love you too, baby. I gotta run." I swear the way she tells me she loves me every time I leave, it's like she knows I'm on some bullshit. She probably does know I'm cheating. I know she loves me and I love her too, but she really not trying to keep us together. I don't even know how we got to this point.

## Meanwhile at Jai's......

Where the hell is this damn Kaseem? He fucking up already and we haven't even been out yet. I know one thing, I didn't get all fly for nothing. I'm giving him 15 - 20 minutes, if he doesn't get here, I'm going to bed. I knew this brother was too good to be true. Most of the time that's how it works.

# Mia

Damn, it's hot out here, it always seems like it's hotter at the airport. I flew to LA to check on my

restaurant, and to see my baby, Jayson Toler. We've been together now for 3 years, and I can honestly say that I

love him. In love with him is a different story, the distance is driving me crazy. Oh shit, I see my baby coming,

with his caramel skin and body like a Greek God. Damn, that nigga fine! That sexy swag got my panties wet as

hell right now. As he walked towards me he said, "Hey, baby, I'm glad to see you. I've missed you so much."

"Jay, you look so good and I miss you too. I want you to come home." I said.

He looked at me, with the most sincere eyes ever, and says,

Babe, I would love to come home, but I need at least another year, until I feel comfortable enough to let

someone else, run my business in my absence."

We grabbed each other's hands and walked towards the baggage claim.

Trying to sound sincere I said, "I know how you feel baby. I was the same way when I opened my second

location out here. You gonna have to learn to trust your employees. I know it sounds

easier than it really is; after all, this is your baby that you started from the ground up. I'm very

proud of you. Baby, it's time to relinquish some responsibility. I thought the point of having your

own business, was to enjoy life more." He seemed to be unbothered by my eagerness to have him with me, for

the sake of us! After grabbing my bags he turned and said, "Well Mia, at least we fly for next to nothing, with

all the frequent flyer miles we racked up."

I'm feeling annoyed now and with slight attitude I said, "Jayson, I'm starting to think that you don't wanna come home to me."

He kissed me on the forehead and said, "Babe, let me take you out on a date tonight."

Then he kissed my cheek so gently, and then slid his tongue across my ear lobe. He knew I couldn't resist. However, his little distraction isn't working for me right now. I agreed to the date, but this convo is far from over. We will be talking about this again. A bitch tired of catching flights and shit! Especially when I don't have to. I remember the first time I saw Jayson again, I was at a college party and he was attending. Howard University summer jam, and he looked just like I had remembered himfrom back in the hood. We automatically had a connection, we came from the same hood and we understood each other. Our relationship didn't last long enough for me to really get to know him, because back then he was busy being a playa and we ended things. It wasn't until after college that, we saw each other at an alumni banquet dinner for our college. He had matured into a great businessman and was trying to start his own business, in marketing and promotions. After playing phone tag for three months, we finally hooked up and it's been three years now. It hasn't been easy either. He had an affair on me and a baby came outta that. I forgave him and we've moved past it. It took a lot for me to trust him again, but I did. I even gave him start up money for his business and things have been ok. When he decided to start the business in LA, it had me feeling insecure a little bit, not knowing what he was doing while I was back in Jersey, but I trusted him to keep his word, he said he'd stay two years. Every time I bring up coming back home, he always got an excuse. So I'm a little annoyed that he thinks he can sweet talk me into not talking about it. Mr. Jayson, this is far from over or we will be over; Trust.

# Meet & Greet

## (Topaz)

I don't know how the fuck, I wound up with Jah again. I guess his charm and that big dick got me hooked, yes big dick! I fucked him on a drunken night out with Jai & Mia at the Strip. We fucked in the VIP room! Yes honey, and it was banging. The drought is over! The night we fucked, he knew I was fucked up. He was the one who kept sending over drinks. I was dancing on the dance floor and the next thing you know, I felt this hard dick against my ass. When I turned to see who it was, it was Jah! We gazed at each other for a second and he whispered in my ear. "Meet me in my VIP room."

I didn't say nothing and actually, he didn't give me a chance to say anything, because he just dipped off. So, I kindly took my ass to bathroom to do a coochie check, and I was straight like an arrow and ready to fuck his brains out! As soon as I walked into the room, he grabbed me around my waist and kissed me like he missed me for real, for real. I was unbuttoning his pants and he was pulling my skirt up! I couldn't wait to feel that dick I felt on the dance floor. I pulled that monster out and I couldn't resist putting that pretty dick in my mouth. As I was sucking the skin off that dick, he was moaning so loud and it turned me on even more. Good thing the music was blasting throughout the club, cause baby it was going down in VIP! He picked me up and carried me over to that little ass table and ate my pussy so good. I almost said, I love you! Now you know the shit good, if you can make a bitch scream that shit and it's ya first time fucking. After he swallowed all my juices, he put that monster inside me and when I tell you, I had an outer body experience, please believe me! Damn, that shit was good. I'm getting wet just thinking about it. After our session, we smoked a blunt and took a couple of more shots and just talked. He finally told me that the night we first met, he was watching me on camera and that's how he knew I was outside smoking. I laughed at that because, I thought it was cute, that he pretended to accidentally run into me. Tonight, we were going out with my girls and their men. Well at least Mia and her man. I don't know about that Kaseem. Something just ain't right about him, but Jai all in love and shit. It seems to me that he always lying about some shit or standing her up. When they have plans, he's always giving her some bogus ass excuse. He's disappointed her so many times already, and it's to the point where this sexy, confident woman is starting to feel insecure and doubting herself. I don't see her smile as much and when she does, it's like she's

pretending to be happy. She's always covering for him, or feeling the need to explain why he does what he does and it's the same shit. He's at work! But hey, if she like it, I love it. I will be watching ole boy though.


**(phone ringing)**


Damnit man, every time I start getting dressed, the damn phone rings.

"Hello, this is Topaz." Still looking in the mirror, I hear this southern voice say,

"Hello, this is your mother."

Aww shit, I forgot I was supposed to call her back to let her know, if I wanted tickets to

her church play. I sat down on the bed to give her a little convo, so she wouldn't be stalking me

all night.

"Hey ma, what's up?"

Sounding relieved I'm giving her a little time she said, "Nothing, what you doing?"

"Actually, I'm trying to get ready to go out for dinner, but the phone just keeps ringing." Hopefully, she got the

hint I just dropped. She paused and continued to say,

"Oh I see, so where you going and with whom?"

I guess not (deep breath) I said, "Just me, Jai, Mia, Jah, Jayson and Kaseem."

"Kaseem? Who is that?" She asked.

I get annoyed just talking about him. I didn't give her any more than she needed to know about him, or we'll be

talking forever. "Oh, that's Jai's new friend." I said.

"Oh really, she can bring him to the play with you and Jah." My mother always trying to get people to come to any church function. Well she's about to be disappointed. I stood up to look at myself again in the mirror, rolling my eyes because I know she's about to be disappointed. I tried to sound just as disappointed as she's about to be and said, "Ma, Jah is not coming. I'm coming by myself, and Jai and Mia already have plans."

"Why Jah not coming? It's a shame that I haven't met him yet."

Here we go again! I told her, "Ma, he has a business to take care of."

"Oh well, if a man don't have time to give to the Lord and thank Him…..

I tuned her out. I don't know what she's saying. I'm trying to think of a way to get out of hearing this sermon.

(beep) Oh thank you Lord, I promise I'll be there on Sunday. She

still talking and I catch the end of her saying…

"And what type of business he conducting on a Sunday?"

I interrupted her, "Ma! Ma! That's my other line, I'mma call you back."

# Jai

"Ok baby, I'll see you there."

Kaseem's meeting is running late, so he'll meet me there. I hate when shit like this happens because Mia and

Erica gone be looking at me sideways once again, and I'm tired of making excuses for him. What I say is truth

and they still be tripping. I can't wait until the renovations are done on his house. I am tired of going to his suite.

I wanna lay up on his sofa and cook in his kitchen and shit. I don't even spend the night over there because, him

and a colleague share this suite. He feels uncomfortable with me sleeping there, with another man sleeping there

too. Especially a man with a key; who can come and go whenever he pleases. Kaseem spends a lot of time at

my house. He spends the night at least 2 nights a month. I'm so not ready for him to be up all in my shit all day,

every day. I love my space  Besides, he has to be at work so early, it just makes sense he stays at his suite

downtown. It's closer to his job.


**(Phone ringing)**


"Hello," I tried sounding sexy.

"Hey poops, you ready?" I just knew it was Kas, but nope it's Mia.

So I said, "Hey Mia, I'm almost ready I just have to do my make up, and then I'm out the door." Mia sounds real

happy tonight. "Ok cool, Jayson and I are bringing wine. I love Savoy's for being ableto bring ya own bottle and

they have a cigar bar, which I think is so cool."

"Ok, I'mma tell Kaseem to stop and pick up a bottle of scotch. I just can't do that wine, it gives me such a headache." I said.

"He's not coming with you?" Mia asked.

"No, his meeting is running a little late, and he'll meet me at Savoy's."

"Ok girl, whatever, just make it!" She said.

"See ya soon, and tell my brother, Jay, I said, 'welcome home.'"

I'm sure he'll get an ear full about Kaseem, if he hasn't already.

# Dinner with a side of "oh shit"

## Topaz

Savoy's is jumping tonight. The lighting is dim and the soft jazz music is nice. The aroma of good food, with a

hint of cigar smoke filled the air, which made me ready for a grown and sexy

evening. I sashayed my ass over to the hostess desk, wearing my sexy little black dress, with the

lace see through front. Jah looked good too, with his all black linen suit and them Red Bottoms

soft soles. That man knows he loves expensive shit. As I walked to the hostess desk I said,

"Good evening, I'm Erica Topaz and I have a reservation."

The waiter facing me, has the prettiest white teeth. He looked me up and down and said,

"Welcome Ms. Topaz, your table is ready and you have guest awaiting your arrival at the bar. Would you like to

be seated now or are you waiting for more guest?"

"I am waiting for more guest, but I would prefer to be seated now, thank you."

The waiter started to escort me, and before I turned to follow I said, "Jah, you can go to the table, and I'm gonna go get Mia and Jayson."

"Ok, but how you know it's them?"

"Because Jai would be by herself, she said Kaseem was running a little late because of a meeting."

The look on Jah's face was like, yeah right! He started asking me questions and said, "What's up with this dude, Topaz? How come Jai can't see this dude full of shit? I tried to hook her up, with my boy, Derek, and she gone say no. Talking about she got a man."

Shaking my head in disbelief. "I don't know baby, but Momma always said, 'what lies in the dark becomes truth in the light.'"

After we are all seated, Kaseem included, we ordered appetizers and sipped on our drinks. The men decided to excuse themselves, and went upstairs to the cigar bar for a little man talk and

cigars.....

# Men Talk

# Jah

Holding up my glass like the boss I am, I tried to get their attention by saying, "Fellas, let's toast to those fine ass women, that we have waiting on us downstairs. My Topaz, and your gems are beautiful, and they all have fat asses! Hahaha, nah but seriously, here's to a nice night, enjoy!" (glasses clinking)

I know this nigga Kaseem and now I'm gonna fuck with him, just to keep him on his toes. I walked over to where he was seated and said, "Ah, that's good shit right there. So Kaseem, tell me something, what you do for a living?"

He looked scared as hell and with his shaky voice he replied, "I'm in marketing."

"Really? Jayson here is in marketing as well. He has his own marketing firm." Laughing on the inside because this nigga really tried to sound excited. He looked at Jayson and said, "Really? That's my ultimate goal. To own my own firm. Hey Jayson, maybe someday we can get together and you school me on some things."

Jayson was busy checking out the women, but he managed to look up and replied, "Sure, we can do that, maybe on my next visit. My home base office is in LA, so I stay out there 10 months outta the year."

Nodding my head in agreement I said, "Ok, that's what's up; brothers helping other brothers build. Me and my partner Anthony can use men like you in our circle. Especially since we plan on opening several businesses."

"Jah, I didn't know you had a partner, every time Mia mentions the club, she only refers to you."

"Really Jayson, I only know Mia through my partner, Tone, I'm surprised you didn't know. They grew up together. They have this brother /sister thing going on since 6th grade! That's what Tone told me."

Jayson is looking surprised as hell but tryna play cool and he don't look so happy but he said,

I'm surprised too, but it's no biggie. I'll ask her about it later."

Jayson gets up and says, "Excuse me fellas, I gotta take me a bathroom break."

Jayson leaves me and Kaseem alone, so now is my chance to ask this nigga for my money. Soon as Jayson was out of earshot, I walked over and said, "So Kaseem, tell me something, when the fuck are you gonna give me my money!?"

"Yo Jah, I told you that I got you. I'm just tryna get all my ducks in order."

I slammed my drink on the table and said, "Ducks in order? The fuck you talking about? You better get me my money, or I'm telling Jai, better yet, I'm telling Topaz and she gone tell Jai. She'll find out that you full of shit and married with 2 kids, my nigga."

Laughing out loud I continued to say, "I see you got your story straight, about what you do for a living. Marketing huh? Good choice."

He got up and moved away from me, like I'm gonna do something to him and said, "Jah, look man, I'mma get your money. I just need a little more time to make shit happen. My people's

just made a run and when he get back, I'mma make some moves and get ya money! On errthang aki."

Through gritted teeth, I looked this nigga straight in his eyes and said, "Aight, but don't think a muthafucker just gone be sitting around trusting ya ass. I'mma be watching and the streets always watching. I want my money in 20 days. That's it and that's all!"

Jayson came back in talking all loud and shit. "Fellas, why y'all looking so tense? What the fuck did I miss?"

"Nothing Jay, we just talking about doing business together one day." I said.

Jayson didn't suspect shit; he was too busy looking at asses. He just grabbed his glass and said,

"Oh ok. Now where's the cigar lady with the big tits and tight ass? I need a light for my cigar."

# Kaseem

"Trina! Come downstairs!" I'm destroying my fucking basement.

"Yeah babe, what's up?" She said

"I put a black bag with a box in it, behind the bar and now I can't find it. Did you move it?"

I'm throwing shit, kicking toys, and tripping over a bunch of bullshit. She waited until I stopped moving shit

and said, "Yeah, I didn't know what it was, so I opened it and found all these guns and so I moved it."

I stopped dead in my tracks. I started to smack her dumb ass but I just said, "Why the fuck wouldn't you tell me

that, when you first found them?! Got me down here going crazy, thinking the boys got to them."

"That's exactly my point, Kaseem! Why would you put that shit in our basement? Where the boys play?"

"It wasn't in their playroom; it was behind the fucking bar!" I said.

"It shouldn't be in the fucking house period! Take that shit to Hak's house. I thought

you said, the run you did last month was your last? I'm not doing another bid, so you better get ya shit

together!"

"Trina, I'm going legit after this run, I had a few loose ends that need to be clipped, in order for me to be right; for us to be right!" I grabbed her by her waist and said, "Listen, I just had a meeting with this guy who owns his own marketing firm out in LA. He's willing to teach me everything he knows about owning my own firm. He got good connects in LA. How you feel about relocating?"

"Humph, it sounds good, but we'll see." She pulled away from my grasp and said, "I will tell you this, I'm not living my life like this anymore. We got little boys and we tryna teach them different! They don't have to grow up rough, like we did. So why put them through jail visits, or gunshot wounds, and the late nights. They wait up for you to come in from the streets. What about me, worrying IF you'll come home! I'm not putting us through any of that anymore."

Only thing I'm thinking about, is getting out this house right now to hurry and finish these deals. I run upstairs and she follows me. I tried to assure her by saying, "I hear you, baby! And just trust me! I gotta run, I'll see you tomorrow."

"Tomorrow?" She said, like she was unaware I was leaving.

"Yeah, I told you I was going to Philly to complete this deal." I said.

"Yeah ok, I'll see you tomorrow. Be safe and come back home in one piece, and without handcuffs. I love you."

# Jai

Fresh sheets on the bed and I'm feeling real fresh myself. I'm so ready for my night with Kas. He's been busy all week working. He promised me a night in Philly, it's one of my favorite cities. Let me call Topaz & Mia now, before they call and be interrupting my night.

**(phone ringing)**

I called Topaz first. She answered, "Hello?"

"Hey Topaz, what's up?" I said.

"Chillin, bout to smoke this L, and get this booty rubbed on."

I laughed and said, "Oh shit now, hold up, let me call Mia."

Mia's ghetto fabulous ass, just gotta be ghetto, and answer the phone like we back down Pennington Court, cooling. She answered and said, "Yerd!"

"Really Mia, this ain't Pennington Court projects, hooker."

"Oh please Jai, just cause we fabulous don't mean I've changed. Hahaha, now what's up?"

"Nothing, I got Topaz on the other end."

(click) I listened to the background before I said, "Hello, Topaz?"

Now, she sounded like she had been hitting the blunt. When she answered she said, "Yeah."

"Hey y'all!, I just wanted to see what my girls were doing. I know Topaz about to get her freak on. What you doing, Mia?"

"Girl, I'm over here writing up a menu for Topaz man and his new restaurant, GEMS. I wonder how he came up with that name?" Waiting for Topaz to give a smart ass answer, but to my surprise, she only said, "oh please bitch, you be knowing."

Mia ain't pay that ass no mind, and continued talking and said, "Mhmm yeah I do, but listen, I'm thinking about having a tasting for him and Tone with a few investors. What you think?"

Topaz ain't correct Mia when she called Jah her man, but I'mma let it slide. Besides, I wanna talk about me, dammit!

"Well Mia, you know anything that is gonna benefit my boo, and his business, I'm fine with." Topaz said.

I started to hang up on these bitches, but then I heard Mia say my name.

"Jai, why you so quiet? The fuck you doing over there?"

"Well Mia, since you asked, I've been a little busy. I'm designing and styling that girl Morgan, from Love and Hip Hop. She's about to go into acting, and do more reality TV shows. Her style is all wrong and her publicist reached out to me, and asked for my assistance. Said she loved my work I did for Tiki Sumpter. Besides, them bitches on Love and Hip Hop be slayed and laid, honey and all by me. So naturally she would ask me to hook her up, and them coins is right honey!"

Topaz love anything involving making money, she shouted through the phone. "I know that's right, bitch! Get that money, honey. So, what's up with sneaky?"

I sucked my teeth hard as hell, because I knew who she was talking about. "Who the fuck is sneaky, Topaz?" I said.

"Jai, you know damn well that, Kas is sneaky as hell."

"Topaz, why would you say that?" I said.

Mia interrupted Topaz before she could answer and said, "Hold up Tee. Let me tell her why WE call him sneaky."

I started rolling my blunt, because I knew they were about to piss me off. Mia continued to say,

"You have never been to his house, or to his office. He only sees you on the weekends, and not every weekend. Y'all only go on group dates, except the first two, and even then, he took you to Philly. It's like he can't be seen with you. Y'all been dating for almost 2 months, how the fuck you don't know his address? Y'all be fucking in hotel rooms and shit, but both of y'all have houses? I know you said that he a boss and the sex is good, but damn bitch, how you let a nigga steal your hood

card? Cause you just overlooking all the signs that the nigga sneaky and lying about something."

"Well damn Mia, tell me how you really feel." I said, feeling annoyed.

"I'm just saying, something ain't right, girl and you know the shit, too."

Topaz puts her two cents in too and said, "Hell, the nigga sound like he married."

I shook my head and put the blunt down and said, "Now Topaz, you know married men don't sleep out at all;

let alone as many times as he does with me. It's Wednesday, not the weekend, and Kas is on his way as we

speak. He will spend the night with me and then we're going to Philly, for a business dinner with his colleges."

I'm feeling good now, and I'm talking shit, too! So, I continued to say, "And we fuck in suites, baby, not a hotel

room like I'm some random hoe. And for the record he took me to his house. The house is being renovated. I

even designed a couple of rooms in the house, you know a woman's touch. All that he hiding me shit, is null

and void." I relit my blunt and took a long pull. I was feeling accomplished in shutting them the fuck up. Mia

knew I was annoyed and gonna reply by saying, "Who said anything about hiding you? Did you, Topaz?  I

know I didn't and so you must have been feeling some kind of way."

"Here you go Mia, I mean Dr. Mia, you always trying to dissect shit." I'm talking with smoke in my mouth and

exhaling out my nostrils. I'm feeling annoyed and I said, "I gotta go, because my man on his way. I love you

bitches, even though y'all get on my last nerve."

(click)

Ugh… I love my girls, but they know how to work my nerves. Let me sip on this wine and get

my mind right. Shit! Where's the other blunt I rolled? I was tryna wait for Kaseem to smoke, but these bitches

all in my head and shit. I'll wait until he gets here and just roll another one.

**(doorbell)**

Yessss, Ddaddy is here. I ran to the door, but not before I stopped and checked myself out in my bedroom

mirror. I opened the door and he stood there looking secy as hell.

"Hey sexy, what's good?"

He was standing in my doorway looking like a tall glass of dark chocolate milk, he smells good, too. When I opened the door, I got a good whiff. I looked in his hands and they were empty.

"Hey daddy, where's your bag?" I said.

He walks in the house, all smooth and shit and said, "My bag?"

"Yeah, I thought you were staying over?"

He kissed me on the cheek, and replied, "Baby, I told you that I had a business trip in Philly. I know I told you that I was leaving tonight."

Ok hold up, and let me think real quick. Now, I know what the fuck he told me. I started raising my voice because I was getting mad right now.

"No, you didn't! You said that you were coming over tonight, and that WE were leaving in the morning TOGETHER, for your meeting!" Throwing my hands up in frustration I said, "I'm getting real tired of this bullshit, you always changing our plans, and half the time you fall through on those, too. What's really going on, Kaseem? I'm far from stupid or naive."

Putting my face in the palms of his hands, he said in a very calm tone, "No one said that you are stupid or naive. I know you're smart and don't nothing get past you."

I'm so not beat for the smooth daddy routine. I got straight to the point. "So, let me ask you this, are you married, with kids? Or living with someone? Do you have a crazy ass baby momma? Because you act sneaky as hell. It's like you hiding me and our relationship. I'm very uncomfortable with that, even got my peoples looking at me sideways."

His demeanor changed, and he moved his hands. He looked around like somebody else was in the house and said, "Hold up! First off, I'm not married! Second, I don't give a fuck about what your boogie ass friends think about me. I'm not fucking them, I'm fucking you."

I think to myself, boogie? Oh! I'mma check him on that one later. Mad as hell now! I started screaming, "Oh! So we just fucking?"

"Jai, that's not what I mean! But don't tell me about what somebody else thinks and feels. How you feel is all that matters, and I don't know about you, but I love you!"

Oh shit! He said he loves me. Damn, should I say it back? I do love him, but... Oh fuck it!

I tilted my head, like I was a little confused and said, "What? You love me?"

He grabbed my face, but this time it felt different. It felt genuine and then he continued to say,

"Yes baby, I do, and even if you don't feel the same way, it doesn't change how I feel."

All I could do was say, "Kaseem Melvin, I love you, too"


**Next Day....**


After last night, I decided to just let Kaseem go to Philly alone. I'm gonna surprise his ass. Let me call into the

office and tell my head assistant Tasha that I changed my plans once again....

"Hello, Jai's Couture." She answered.

"Hey Tash, this is Jai. I'mma need you to go over to the photo shoot. The one I'm supposed to be styling today.

All the looks are in the portfolio on my desk. The wardrobe is packed and ready to go in the lab." (That's

where I store all the wardrobes for photo shoots) "I'm going to Philly, and won't be back until tomorrow. I've

already called the client and they're expecting you. I'll forward all the business calls to your phone, as they

come in. Do a great job and you know, I trust you if I'm sending you. Don't worry you got this."

"Philly? You going to Philly, again? You love it out there, let me find out you trying to open another business

out there and gone leave poor Tasha here."

I was throwing clothes in an overnight bag, because my flight leaves in an hour. As I zipped

my bag, I looked around to make sure I packed everything and I said, "Girl no, I'm going out there to surprise

my boo. Trust me honey, if I was to open another spot in Philly, you are coming with! I couldn't manage

without you." I checked my watch and realized I've been talking too long, I ended the convo quickly and said,

"I gotta run, have a great shoot and remember have fun. Ain't nothing like doing what you love to do. So, enjoy

and call me if anything, and I mean, if anything happens that I should know about."

I hung up too fast, but I think I heard her say, "Ok, Jai have a great time."

# MIA

With excitement in my voice I said, "Good morning gentlemen and how are you this fine morning?" Jah held the door open for me as I entered my office where he, Tone, and two other investors were waiting for me. Tone was standing there with his business face on.

"Oh, cut the shit. Mia, what's good with it? How we looking for this tasting? Because we are ready to rock out."

I looked at Tone over the top of my glasses, like I was his teacher and said, "Ok, Mr. Anthony Jackson, or should I just refer to you as Tone?"

He smirked like he was digging my style and said, "Hahaha, come on now stop playing and let's get to business."

"Ok, how's Friday at the Savoy Bar and Lounge? I can reserve a room for us."

Jah turned and looked up at me from his phone and said, "Why there? Shit, you gone pay them? We can do it at The Strip, for free! It would have to be a weekday, though. The nights and weekends are strictly for partying."

"Ok that's fine, I only chose Savoy's because I knew your parties are on nights and weekends. I just assumed you guys wanted it to be at night. I'm cool with wherever and whenever you guys choose. So how about, we do it on a Wednesday or Thursday? Whichever is better for you guys. I need a date today, though."

I was waiting for Tone's response because, he was supposed to be going away. He chimed in first because he knew the shit.

"Let's do it on Wednesday, because I'm going away that weekend and leaving Thursday morning."

I thought to myself, good choice, negro! Jah second his choice and I agreed by saying, "Wednesday is fine for me, as well. If everyone's on board, we can meet there at 3pm and I'll explain each dish as it's being served. You can tell me what you like and what you don't like."

The meeting was quick, and I told them I had another meeting to take. As I gathered my belongings, the investors were sticking around as if they waiting for me to leave. This is my office so, what they waiting on? I started moving a little faster, but then Tone changed all that. He must have peeped me getting annoyed. He walked over towards the men, and with his hands he gestured them out the door.

"Ok fellas, I'll meet you at The Strip tonight. Excuse me, while I talk to Ms. Mia for a second, I need to speak with her on another matter."

As the fine ass brothers walked out the meeting, I'm thinking, shit! They fine as hell! If I didn't have a man, I would be flirting my ass off and seducing them with my food. As soon as the door closed, he grabbed me by my waist, and pulled me in real close. He kissed my lips and whispered, "You ready for our trip next weekend?"

"Tone! This is my place of business, and my assistant can walk in at any given time."

Looking in those beautiful brown eyes, I continued to say, "Yes honey, I'm ready and can't wait."

He went from 0 to 100 real quick and said, "Dammit Mia, I'm tired of this sneaking shit! You need to leave ole pretty boy alone. He don't deserve you. How can a man leave a beautiful woman, like you alone for weeks at a time and think that's ok?"

He walked away from me and sat in one of my guest seats. Trying to make the energy shift, I said, "I know babe, and I'm tired, too." I walked over and sat next to him and placed my hands on top of his lap and said, "I'm not happy with him anymore. Even when he visits, I don't wanna be bothered. The last time he was here, we went to the Savoy Lounge for dinner. I know you know, cause your boy Jah told you. In any case, once we got home, he questioned me about you. He wanted to know the extent of our relationship." I saw his demeanor change real quick, when I said that.

"What the fuck made him ask you that?"

"I don't know, something about Jah mentioning his business partner, and how you and I were real close like, brother and sister, and how I'm supposed to be head chef, and ect, ect."

In a calm voice now he said, "Oh ok, but you know I don't give a fuck right? I wish he would find out, so he can leave."

"I'm done anyway. I think I'mma take a quick flight out to LA, and break it off. This long distance shit ain't working. Especially since I'm in love with you."

"Why you gotta go out there, though?"

I gave him a little peck on the lips and said, "because it's a coward move, to break up over the phone. I can at least do it the right way. I don't hate him. I just fell outta love with him, and in love with my "brother". Hahaha, and besides that, no way in hell he out there and not fucking random bitches when he get horny."

I laughed and Tone made a joke about our so called brother/sister relationship and he said,

"Imma show you motherfucking brotherly love too! Hahaha."

"You crazy man!" I said.

He grabbed me by the waist again, and this time tighter and said,

"Yup, crazy about yo fine ass. Can I kiss you now?"

I smiled and said, "mhmm, come here, baby."

# KASEEM

I'm sitting in Hak's house, tryna get shit right with him and hoping that he really listens to what

I'm tryna offer him. "Listen Hak, I came out here to make a deal and you tripping."

"Nah nigga, you trippin! You owe 50k and you bringing me these bullshit ass guns, like I'mma take that shit."

He pushed the bag off the table with his feet and continued to say, "I didn't give you fucking guns and tell you

to sell them when you asked me for 50k, did I?" He banged the hell out that table, making shit fall over. He

asked me again, "Did I, nigga?"

"No, but I can't move shit outta the bricks. Tone and Jah got the shit on lock. Once Jah and'em found out I was

tryna push my shit, they made me pay a fine of 50k, too or I was gonna get pushed. Shit! I can't get both of y'all

that money, at the same damn time. They stopped my business and my connects ain't fucking with me since I

paid them what I owed them." Sipping and shaking my head at the same damn time. I continued to say, "Shiiid,

I got a wife and kids

to take care of, too."

"Nigga, I don't give a fuck about none of that bullshit you talking. My only concern is my

fucking money. You got 60 days to run me my shit. I don't give a fuck how you get it, just get me my money,

before I put interest on the shit!" He stopped what he was doing for a second, laughed and said, "Hahaha, now

get my shit, or Mrs. Melvin gonna be looking for a black dress and suits for them boys."

Damn! I'm looking like yo; this my boy. We use to eat oodles and noodles out the same fucking bowl when we was knocked off. He talking to me like I'm some buster ass nigga! With my head slanted I said, "Word Hak, you really going to threaten my family, nigga?"

He hesitated cause, this nigga knew he was wrong. He gotta save face in front of his flunkies, but it's cool.

"Nah nigga, just yo ass. Just run me my shit, and take them guns back to papi and'em. I don't want them shits," he said.

Shaking my head, I just picked the bag up and said, "Aight look, I got this side chick who all in love and shit, but her paper long and I'mma get it from her." I know it's fucked up, but shit, I gotta do what I gotta do and Jai gone help me.

"I don't give a fuck who or where, just run me my shit, and you got 60 days or I'm coming for you!"

I grabbed the bag and walked towards the door, checking out every goon's face. Just in case I need them for anything. "Aight, I got you. I think it's real fucked up, you coming for me like this. I thought we were cool."This nigga Hak, turned his back and walked away from me.

"We cool, nigga, but this business! Peace." He said.

# <u>Jai</u>

I know this the hotel. We always stay here when we come to Philly. That damn winch at the front desk, wouldn't give me the room number that Kas is staying in. She wouldn't even tell me if he's registered here. That's some bullshit and I didn't see his car in the lot as I was pulling in.

I'mma just check in and wait for him in the lobby. I should grab a drink at the bar, this way I won't miss him. After checking in, I grabbed my bag and went into the bar and ordered something to eat and a drink. While eating my grilled chicken salad and sipping my wine, I felt this warm air across the back of my neck. When I turned around, my baby Kas, was standing there. He was looking good and smiling, like he was happy to see me. I smiled and said,

"Well, I see somebody's happy to see me. SURPRISE baby!"

He kissed the top of my head, and sat down next to me and said, "And what a great surprise it is, baby. "I'm glad you're here. I thought you were gonna stay home and work this weekend?"

"Well, when you the boss, you can travel whenever you feel like it. So, I decided to surprise my baby."

He took a piece of chicken off my plate and said, "I see you're eating already, so I'll order something and have lunch with you."

Looking at his face, I see something is wrong. I asked him, "Baby are you ok? You look stressed."

He continued picking chicken off my plate and said, "I'm ok, just a little set back. It'll all work out."

"You sure? If there's anything I could do, just let me know." I said.

"Yeah, I'm sure, I just gotta get my mind right and come up with a marketing plan, my investor can't refuse. Thanks for your support, and if I need you, I'll be sure to let you know," he said.

"How you know I was here?" I said.

"The lady at the front desk told me, there was a woman waiting for me at the bar."

"Well, at least she can follow directions, because she was giving me a hard time."

With a raised eyebrow he said, "Oh was she, now? Well I'mma make a complaint, no one gives my baby a hard time." Aww look at my boo, standing up for me. I so love this man.

He continues to say, "How about we get this food sent to the room, and you can eat up there?"

"What about your food? Aren't you gonna eat?" I said.

With a raised eyebrow, he says, "Oh I'mma eat alright, YOU!"

I quickly got up and gestured for the waiter and said, "Now that's what I'm talking about! I'mma go cancel my room and you have the food sent."

He stepped back, and watched me walk away and said, "Ok, let's go."

# Topaz

I'm kicking back with my feet on Jah's desk at The Strip. I'm enjoying my blunt, and my bottle of Moet, that Jah had sent up. I'm just watching the comings and goings of the patrons on the hidden cameras. I see Jah and Tone outside talking, and this dude who doesn't look like he belongs in this club, walked up looking like he needed crack or some shit. From the looks of this, it looked like Jah and Tone were not pleased about whatever is being said. Damn, you would think, with all this high tech shit he got going on in here, the camera would have sound. The convo was short and the man stepped off. Jah was on his way back inside, he was probably on his way up here. Let me put my shoes back on before he comes in here, thinking that I think, I'm the boss. Just as I put on my shoes, he came in smiling, and kissed my lips.

"Hey, my queen, what you up here doing? Oh, I see the waitress brought you that bottle, and I smell it in the air. So, you just up here chillin like a boss?"

"I am a boss baby." I said.

Smiling like he really agrees with me, he said, "yes you are, but you good though?"

I nodded and said, "yeah, just being nosy. I saw you and Tone out there talking. Who was the dude who walked up to y'all looking like a crackhead?"

He started reaching in his drawer, avoiding eye contact. Meaning he about to lie his ass off. He looked at me and looked away real fast and said, "That was one of my old workers begging and pleading his case. We fired his ass from the kitchen for stealing," he said.

"Oh damn, maybe he needed the food, baby. He didn't steal money, did he?"

"Only because he didn't have access to it. Trust me, his crack head ass would've, if

he could've. One thing I can't stand is a thief and he my peoples. If he really needed food for his family, all he had to do was ask me and he knows, I would've given it to him." He paused for a minute like, he was disappointed and continued to say, "Don't steal from me, point blank and period."

Damn, this conversation made him angry. It's gotta be deeper than what he's telling me. Trust me, I'll find out, what lies in the dark becomes truth in the light. Time to switch this up and get my baby's mind focused back on me! I stood up and walked over to him with my sexy walk.

"Come here, daddy, and give me some sugar. I want you to watch me on those cameras. I'm about to go shake my ass. Can you please tell the DJ to play Jersey club classics?"

He stood up and met me at the door and gave me the sweetest kiss. "Aight, baby, you got it and trust me, I will be watching that ass. Have a great time and I'll be down there as soon as I smoke this blunt." He slapped me on my ass and I chuckled and went downstairs.

**(The Next Week)**

It's been a long ass weekend and I'm tired as hell. No more clubbing for me; for a long while.

I need a strong coffee this morning. I hope Dee's at his desk now. "Dee, coffee please, with a double shot."

"Double shot of what?" He said.

I sucked my teeth and replied, "Really, Dee? I wish it was Henny. Just bring me my usual, but add a double shot of espresso, and please bring in Shane's article from the edit box, thanks."

"Yes, ma'am," he said.

I hate when he calls me ma'am and he knows that shit.

**(knock, knock)**

Before I could say come in, Dee just walked in talking all loud and shit, calling me ma'am.

"Next time, wait until I say come in, and stop calling me, ma'am. We're almost the same age."

He placed the coffee in my hand and sucked his teeth. "Oh honey, please hurry up, and drink this coffee, cause you funky this morning. It's all that partying, I saw your ass at The Strip last weekend. You was shaking that fat ass, with that fine ass piece of Chocolate."

I sipped my coffee and leaned back in my chair and said, "Yasss honey, and that piece of chocolate belongs to me."

Giving me the side eye and sucking his teeth he said, "Yeah, I can tell. You made sure all the women knew he was yours! Here's that fine."

He placed the folder on my desk and asked me, "Oh, and since when you started liking bad boys?"

"I always liked a little bad boy in my men. But he is a recovering bad boy, making legit moves."

"Ok now, I know that's right, honey." Dee said.

As he walked towards the door, he turned and said, "Is there anything else I can get for you, Ms. Topaz, because my boss keeps me really busy. I don't have time to be kicking it with you."

I used my hand to shoo him away like a bird and said, "No that's all, thanks, boo."

I love my gay assistant, he's the bomb dot com. As I opened the folder, all I could

think was, Shane's been trying to get me to read and approve this article since forever. Let's

see what he's got. I'll give any good writer a shot at a cover story, if it's good enough. He wants

to do a serious piece because he's tired of writing puff pieces. In other words, little shit to fill up

the pages. Hmmm, let's see, the title is interesting.


**"Reformed and Legit: From Street King to Legit King"**


Now, that title has my attention!

# **Mia**

I was looking out the window, feeling excited and sad at the same time. On one hand, I'm

breaking up with Jayson, but on the other hand, I get a bomb ass massage and a damn good

margarita. The pilot came over the loudspeaker, "Good evening, this is your pilot, Captain Fitz. I would like to

welcome you all, to Los Angeles. Please enjoy your stay in sunny California."

Looking out the window and damn, it's beautiful out here. I love LA. That's why I had to have me a restaurant

out here. It also gave me a reason to come out here, at least twice a year to check on business. Since Jay's been

out here, I come even more than expected. I probably should have called him first, to let him know I was

coming out here. I just felt like if I did, I would have to tell him why and no one wants to hear, 'we gotta talk'

over the phone. Naturally, it will turn into an argument about what it is and why I need to come to LA to talk,

Yada, yada, yada. That's the shit I'm trying to avoid, so I made reservations at the Laguna Suites. They make the best margaritas ever, and the spa is to die for. After the talk with Jayson, I'mma need both. I miss Tone though, let me call him and let him know that I landed. I started unpacking while the phones was ringing. Hmmmm.. He must be busy, if it's going to voicemail. I left a voice message and said, "Hey babe, I landed safely and I'm about to relax at the spa and talk to Jay tomorrow, call me back though. I love you, bye."

(The Next Day)

I had a great night. I had a couple of margaritas and a full body massage. I guess I'll start preparing for dinner tonight with Jay. Soon as I reached for my cell, it started ringing and it was Jayson.

"Hello, sunshine," he said.

Like a little girl, I sat straight up and fixed my hair. I felt like he could see me.

"Hey Jay, what you doing? Have you left for work yet?" I said.

"Yes, I'm actually sitting at my desk now. What's up beautiful?"

"You never call me in the mornings. Is everything ok?" I said.

He replied with confidence. "Yes, everything is fine. Just wanted to talk."

Sounds like he misses me, so it shouldn't be a problem seeing him today.

"You think you have time for me today?" I said.

Sounding like he was grinning, "I always have time for you and if I don't, I'll make time. What's up, baby? You sound so blah."

Without answering him I just asked, "How about I meet you for dinner?"

Sounding surprised he asked, "Dinner? You flying out?"

Sitting up looking for my lighter, I said, "I'm actually here already, I landed yesterday." I don't think I ever heard Jay be lost for words. Right now he really seems like he's surprised, but not in a good way.

"Oh, wow baby, why didn't you tell me you were coming? Where you staying? Oh never mind, I know your spot. Did you enjoy the spa treatments and the margaritas?" This man knows, he knows me so well.

"Yes, you know I did. So, dinner tonight?" I replied.

Sounding more like himself, he says, "Sure babe. I'll call you when I'm leaving the office. Are you sure you're ok? You don't sound like my Mia."

I lit my blunt, and took a long pull before I said, "Yes, I'm fine. I'll see you later."

When I hung up, I started thinking. I don't think this conversation should happen at a restaurant, especially mine. We usually dine there when I come in town. It gives me a chance to see the operation of my business and to make sure the food is up to my standards. Tonight though, is not the best time. I'll come in to check on things before I return home.

# Girl Talk 2

# Mia

**(phone ringing)**

"Hello, this is Topaz."

"Hey girl, what's up?" I said. Topaz picked up on it right away and said, "Hey Mia, what's wrong? I can tell something's up by the way you said, 'Hey girl.'"

Laying across my bed, still smoking my blunt I said, "Call Jai on the three way. I gotta tell y'all something."

She paused like she wanted to ask me something, but changed her mind and just told me to hold on.

Topaz said, "Hello?"

"My bad Tee, I was sipping my margarita, even though it's 10 am!" I said.

Jai was on the phone now and she said, "10am? Where are you?"

Sitting Indian style on the bed smoking I said, "I'm in LA, I came out here to talk to Jay."

Jai acting like I planned a girls' trip without her and said, "Damn Mia, you could've told a bitch. I could use some fun in the sun."

"Trust me Jai, this ain't a pleasure trip." I said.

Jai paused for a minute, and no one said anything. After complete silence Jai said, "Damn Topaz, you're right, something is up. Spill the tea bitch, what's up?"

"Ok first, don't y'all start tripping, and getting all in your feelings about what I'm going to tell you."

Topaz interrupted me by saying, "Mia, it's me and Jai, of course we gone be in our feelings, or it wouldn't be us."

Jai co-signed what Mia responding, "yea Mia, you know us, but spill the tea dammit! I have to meet Kas for lunch today at Savoy's. Yes! Us outside, by ourselves, being seen."

Topaz not feeling the Kaseem talk and quickly cut Jai off and said, "Bitch please, fuck what You talking about. What's wrong, Mia?"

"I came to LA to break up with Jayson." I said.

"What? Why, Mia?" Jai said.

"Because Jai, it just ain't the same. The distance and now he talking about extending his stay out here and you know what? He never asked me if I would move out here to make us work. It was always me, asking him to come home. I feel like, it was a one sided relationship." I said. Shrugging my shoulders in uncertainty, I continued to say, "Don't get me wrong, I think he loves me, and I love him and I always will. But our time has ended. Honestly, I don't think he is in love with me anymore."

"Mia, are you in love with Jay anymore?" Topaz asked.

I relit my blunt and went out on the balcony to smoke. After giving it some thought I said, "Topaz, to be honest no, and I haven't been in a long time. I'm in love with Anthony."

Oops! That just came out of nowhere. I'm about to get a thousand and one questions now. Jai yelled loud as hell into the phone.

"Who the fuck is Anthony?"

In shock, Topaz says in a calm voice, "Wait! You in love with Tone?"

Here goes Jai, thinking somebody keeping shit from her, and she says, "How you know Topaz? And I don't? Mia, you got some explaining to do."

Before Jai started some shit that don't exist, let me clear this shit up right now.

"Topaz didn't know Jai, she knows his real name because her man and him are partners."

Shaking my head in exhaustion, because now Topaz getting in her feelings too and gone say,

"So Jahmar knew, and didn't tell me?"

Again, I'm explaining shit. I said, "Erica he didn't know, nobody knew."

Topaz started laughing and said, "I knew you was fucking that nigga! Talking about he ya brother and shit. How long y'all been fucking around?"

Taking a deep breath, I said, "Now y'all don't trip, but we been together for 8 months."

Again, Jai yelling in the damn phone, saying, "8 fucking months, Mia! For real and you ain't say shit to us? My fucking feelings hurt!"

"Jai, I wasn't trying to hurt you or Topaz's feelings. I know y'all love Jayson." I said.

Topaz was still talking in a calm voice, she must be high as hell. She said, "yeah, but Mia, we love you more and it's always gonna be about whatever makes you happy."

"Thanks, Topaz." I said.

Jai was still tripping and talking loud and said, "fuck that, I'm still mad, bitch!"

Topaz started laughing and said, "bitch you always mad, get over it!" Topaz continued, "so Mia, did you tell him yet?"

Walking over to the hotel's mini fridge to get my drink from last night, I said, "no! That's why I'm drinking margaritas at 10 in the morning. I'm nervous and I don't wanna hurt him. I think he feels the same way. He just don't know how to end things. So I'll do it for us both."

Jai laughed and said, "well bitch, you better than me, because I would have sent an email, or a long ass text."

"Jai, I would never! I don't hate Jayson. I just think we just fell out of love." I said.

Topaz ended the convo by saying, "well, call us when it's over, we love you, girl."

Jai responded, "yeah, good luck, Mia and I'm still mad, bitch!"

Laughing out loud I said, "whatever, I love y'all, too. I'mma call y'all."

# Jayson Carter

"Nancy, get Sam on the phone for me, please."

I'm packing up and getting ready to go because I have dinner plans tonight. My secretary, Nancy, interrupted my train of thought by buzzing the phone and saying, "Mr. Carter., I have Sam on line 1."

I stopped what I was doing and picked up the phone and said, "Hey babe, how are you?"

"I'm fine, baby. Are you ok?"

"Yes, but I'mma have to cancel our plans for dinner tonight. Mark is having trouble with one of our biggest clients. He asked me to meet with them to seal the deal, and as much as I wanna be with you, looking at your pretty face. I have to sit across a table and stare at a big burly man."

I laughed at that thought and she responded, "oh baby, that's alright. I'll just go home and finish some work. I'll have your dessert waiting for you. It's called, Samantha ala mode."

Smiling and rubbing my dick I said, "you know that's my favorite, don't forget the whipped cream."

With a devilish laugh she said, "haha, do I ever? I'll see you later baby, my class is starting."

Kissing the phone, I said, "ok love, I love you."

"I love you more," she said.

# Mia & Jayson

# (The End)

Ok, I look nice but not sexy. I have my wine and food to prepare, time to hit the road.

I pray this goes well, I told Jayson to meet me at my restaurant at 8pm. This way I know he'll go

home first to change or freshen up. I'll be there already, waiting for him with dinner made.

It's sad and I hate to say it, but I miss him already. This may be the last time I see him.

Although it's difficult, it's the best thing for us both. I jumped in the car, with groceries for dinner, and a bottle

of wine, turned up the music and rode out. Why must I listen to Mary on my way to break up with Jayson? This

shit making me sad. I'mma have to have this car detailed before I take it back to the rental office. I'm about to

smoke this blunt and get my mind right. First I gotta change this music, where's my Gucci Mane? Looking in

the glove box, I find it. I popped it in and started rapping the lyrics, "*starting my day with a blunt of purp, no pancakes just a cup of syrup."* Yasss, now that's what I'm talking about, some ride out music. I parked in the

parking garage and I didn't see Jayson's car. Which means he's not here yet.

# Samantha Durant

# (Sam)

I walked towards the door and see one of my favorite people, Bernie the doorman, and right

away he greets me and says, "good evening, Ms. Durant."

"Please Bernie, call me Samantha, or Sam. How many times do I have to tell you, my mother is Ms. Durant."

"Yes ma'am, I mean, Ms. Samantha," he said.

# Jayson

Just as I was leaving, my secretary stopped me and said, "Mr. Carter, Mark asked that you stop by his office before you leave."

"Ok, thanks, Nancy." I said.

Damn! I used his ass as an excuse, didn't think it would really happen, sheesh. I hope this don't take long, I got shit to do.

# Mia

Driving towards this building, had me reminiscing. I remembered the first time I laid eyes on this 42 Story, beautiful building, I knew I would love this condo. Valet parking and a doorman. I knew this was a perfect spot when Jayson and I decided to buy it. It fit him perfectly. Walking into the building. Bernie, the doorman is grinning from ear to ear. "Good evening, ma'am."

"Good evening, Bernie, how are you?"

Holding the door open for me he says, "I'm good Ms. Lawson. How long will you be staying this trip?"

As I walked through the door, I nodded and passed him a five-dollar tip and said, "Oh Bernie, I don't know, but it's always a pleasure to see you."

"Thank you, ma'am. Enjoy your evening." He said.

After talking with Bernie, I got off the elevator and started thinking that this was the walk of death, at least that's what it feels like. It kinda is the death of our relationship. He'll probably change the locks after tonight, but I'll leave the keys. This way it will save him the trouble of having the locks changed. Somebody about to turn up tonight. I hear music blaring and then I started thinking, oh shit, he must have beat me here. That music I hear, is coming from Jayson's apartment. He in there jamming to R Kelly's, "Black Panties". I hope he not in there thinking we fucking after dinner. That is not happening, or is it? I mean, I could have some break up sex. That nigga know that he knows how to lay it down. Well, here goes nothing, I put the key in the door and quietly turn the knob, tryna surprise him. Damn! Did I get an eye full of some bullshit? I started yelling at the top of my lungs,"Bitch, who the fuck are you?"

She stopped her little two step dance and said, "who are you? And how you get in here?"

Dropping the bags in the middle of the floor I said, "bitch, first off, put some fucking clothes on in my fucking house!"

This bitch walking around in this skinny ass G string, with no fucking ass, and big ass titties. Looking like she paid a grip for them unnatural shits. She covered herself and said, "your house?"I put my hands on my hips and rolled my eyes and said, "yes, bitch! My fucking house, and where the fuck is Jayson?" I'm looking around the house like, I know this bitch not in here by herself. Then I found myself repeating shit. I turned the music off and said, "I'm his fiancé, and I'm not gonna tell you again, to put some fucking clothes on in my fucking house!"

Still standing there, like a deer in headlights she says, "oh my God! His fiancé? How is that possible when I'm his wife?!"

I damn near passed out!

# Jayson

Bernie looks extremely happy tonight. He's smiling real hard, maybe he finally fucked that old

rich lady on the 34th floor. As I approached the door, Bernie opened it wide and said, "Evening Mr. Carter, you

having a busy night tonight, huh?"

Walking through and shaking his hand I said, "evening Bernie, what do you mean?"

"Well, Mr. Carter, both misses are here tonight." He said.

"What?" I said.

"Yes sir, Ms. Durant and Ms. Mia, sir." He said.

Looking down both ends of the hallway like they gonna jump out on me I said, "Oh shit! Are you sure?"

"Yes sir, I let them both in." Bernie said.

"You did what? Why the fuck would you do that?"

Bernie sounded like, he was annoyed and he said in a calm, but in a matter of fact kinda way.

"Sir, my job is to open and close doors, nothing more and nothing less."

I felt bad for talking to him like that and I said, "you're right, Bernie. I'm sorry. How the fuck this happen?

What should I do?"

Staring at Bernie, praying he had answers. All he did was look out the tall glass doors and said,

"I don't know, sir."

Fuck it! It was bound to happen; I just didn't want it to go down like this. I fixed my clothes

out of nervousness and picked up my briefcase and asked him, "Bernie, how long ago did you let them in?"

"About a half an hour ago." He said.

I panicked and shouted, "Half an hour! And no police were called?"

Bernie looking scared and said, "no, sir."

I stood there for a minute, thinking, shit, shit, shit! That means they either killed each other, or…. oh hell, who am I fooling? Mia will kill Sam; I better get up there. I reached in my pocket and said, "Bernie, do me a favor please. Take this $100 and come up to my apt. in 15 minutes just to make sure everything's ok, I'll let you know what to do once you get there."

I hauled ass to the elevator, praying they still alive.

# Mia

I'm sitting on the couch, like a straight thug. Legs open wide enough to catch my balance, in case I gotta jump up and smack a bitch, my feet will be firmly planted. I looked at this bitch and said, "Ok Ms. Samantha, let me get this straight, you've been married to Jayson for how long?"

I'm really trying not to smack this bitch as she stands there looking unbothered. She started talking in this valley girl accent and said, "well, we're not actually married, I was just trying to one up you. We've been together for one and a half years. I never knew anything about you, he has never mentioned you before."

Shaking my head and as bad as it hurts, I can't drop no tears. I'm too mad. I just kept saying, "one and half years! That summabitch! Oh, all hell's gonna break loose when that nigga

get in here tonight."

She finally has clothes on and sat across from me on the loveseat. She had the nerve to ask me a dumb ass question.

"You want some wine, Mia?"

"Hell fucking, no! I don't want no damn wine! This ain't no damn party, bitch. It's gonna be a damn funeral!" I started pointing my fingers at her and said, "I tell you one thing you can have, and that's his

sorry, piece of shit, ass. I only came out here to break up with him. I knew something wasn't right."

Crossing her legs like she real comfortable, she asked me, "Mia, if you don't mind me asking, but how long

were you two together?"

She's really sitting there like this a sister to sister conversation. She actually poured herself a cocktail, like we

on vacation. I really wanna know some shit, so I'mma be cool and get what info I need from her.

I answered her with disappointment in my voice and I said, "Jayson and I have been together for 3 years, and

engaged for one year."

As I'm talking, I'm getting even more mad and I'm thinking, this some straight bullshit. I'mma kill this nigga,

and that's my word! He got me all the way fucked up! All the traveling I've been doing, all the time and money

I spent. He better find himself another cosigner for this condo, or his ass gone be homeless, I'm taking my name

off this shit. I'm the one who helped him start that business. All the sacrifices I made for this no good, cheating

ass, liar, I'mma kill him! Now I need a fucking drink. I looked at her with the side eye, and she was entirely too

calm for my liking. She looked at me and said, "You want that wine now?"

"No bitch, I don't want no fucking wine, I want a real fucking drink. Go get me a shot of the tequila in the

liquor cabinet."

Like the good little bitch, she is, she got up to go and get me a fucking glass and says, "ok, I'll be right back."

Why this bitch acting like everything good? She funny money and I think this bitch knew about me. She came

back with a glass in hand, and says, "here you go."

I looked at the glass real suspect like and said, "No, you drink it." I moved her hand out my face. I don't know

if she put something in my shit. So, I drank from the

bottle. After a nice big gulp, I started asking questions. "So, tell me something, why you so fucking calm? You

acting like you knew about me and shit."

"I promise you, I knew nothing about you, Mia. I'm not going to get myself upset over a man, whom I don't

love. He treats me well, and I love his money, and how he takes care of me. Clearly you love him, and I feel bad

he's done this to you. I'm not that invested in the relationship."

Did this bitch just straight let me know that she a hoe? I took another big gulp. She can't be fucking serious, I had to ask for clarity. I sat back because, I drank too fast and needed the back support and I said, "So, you fucking and sucking for money?"

"Yup, and he pays my tuition for school." She said.

Shit! I ain't even mad about her hustle. I'm from the hood, so I see the shit all the time. Damn, but why my man? Feeling good from the shots of tequila I said, "well, he should be on his way here."

She gon' have the nerve to say, "I don't think so, because we were supposed to have dinner, but he's in a meeting."

Now, I'm looking at her with the, you so fucking stupid look. Laughing out loud and I said,

"nah, Samantha, he told you that because we had dinner plans. What he didn't plan on, was me waiting for him here instead of my restaurant."

"Oh, you have a restaurant?" She asked.

Feeling proud that I'm not her, and fucking for money. I started bragging. "Yes, I do, the 420 Bar and Grill."

"Wow! We eat there all the time. He said his long time, childhood friend, Jay owns it." Sam said.

"I own the restaurant, but he used my sister's name and said she owned it. I guess he was covering his ass, just in case. I don't know, nor do I care, but that's my shit."

"Wow, he's just a liar," she said, with surprise.

I'm sitting here thinking, I can't believe he brought his side chick to my shit. She started talking and I Heard her say, "he was playing both of us!"

That shit pissed me off, and I started yelling and said, "bitch, please! He was playing me, clearly you just in it for the money." I got up and started towards the kitchen and said, "whelp, might as well start cooking dinner. We can all eat like one big happy family."

Ole girl looking at me like I'm crazy and I am!

"Wait, you gonna cook in the middle of this situation?"

"Yes, the fuck I am, a bitch high and hungry, you smoke?" I said. I really don't want or need an answer to that, but she responded anyway. Good, I'mma put this bitch to work. I sat down and passed her the knife and said, "ok, miss Samantha, chop this onion while I roll this blunt. Mr. Carter is gonna have his ass a good last meal."

As I laid my blunt down, I heard the elevator buzzer and what sounded like the elevator doors. That nigga prolly scared shitless. Scared Molly over there, acting like somebody about to die. She says,"oh shit! I think he's coming, Mia."

Why is she standing behind the wall, as if I'mma shoot his ass or something? These chicks are scary as hell, you can tell she ain't from the hood. I looked at her ass and said, "good, I'm waiting on that ass."

I heard his ass turning the door knob all easy and shit. I'm sure Bernie's ass told him, both his bitches is here. As I lit my blunt, I took a long pull, inhaled that shit, and exhaled through my nostrils. He's turning the corner and as soon as we made eye contact, I said with a grin on my face, "Hey daddy, why you ain't tell me you like white bitches?!"

He looked around for his scary white bitch and he asked me, "Mia, what are you doing here?"

Scary Sam came from around the kitchen counter and says, "No Jayson, what the fuck are you doing here?"

He looked relieved and scared at the same damn time. "Sam! I can explain." He said.

I was shooting daggers with my eyes. If looks could kill, he'd be a dead motherfucker, I started yelling in his face and said, "Sam? The fuck you mean, Sam? You should be explaining shit to me."

He backed up out of fear of me fucking him up and said, "Mia, I wanted to tell you but…"

"But what, Jayson? You been fucking this white bitch for over a fucking year! Playing house and shit! Taking this bitch to my restaurant, and you gave her a key, to the place that my name is on and you been meaning to tell me? Fuck you! You fucking bastard!" Pointing my finger in his face, I was on the verge of slapping him. "And how the fuck you paying her tuition for school, but won't pay fucking child support for your kid you had on me 2 years ago?"

Oh shit! That bit of info got the white bitch's attention. She turned her head around so fast and said, "kid? What kid?" Samantha said.

"Oh Ms. Samantha, he's done this shit before. He cheated on me with some other bitch and had a baby. I guess this time, he had a taste for some white pussy."

I lit my blunt, and she turned to him and said, "Jayson, you didn't tell me you had a kid."

I think it's funny, because he acts like she's not standing there talking to him. I'm not gone even blow her cover about her using him for cash, not now anyway. "Of course not, darling, he's not telling you that. That would taint his '*good man*' image. In reality, he ain't shit!" I shouted.

I'm laughing on the inside because, this chick about to be mad. A baby getting her coins, hahaha, I laughed to myself at the turmoil he about to go through, and with a bitch he thinks loves him. He standing there looking stupid as fuck, not saying shit and I'm tired of this standoff shit. I asked him, "what the fuck? Cat got ya tongue? You don't have shit to say, huh?"

He bowed his head like he ashamed and whispered, "I'm sorry."

That did it! I completely lost it. I jumped up out my seat and slapped the dog shit out his ass. Ole girl was screaming and shit, I snapped my head around and looked at her and said, "Shut the fuck up, bitch! Sit yo ass down somewhere!"

Jayson was standing there, holding the side of his face with tears in his eyes. When I saw that I said, "oh bitch, you crying? Did I hurt you? I'm not done! First thing tomorrow, I'm calling the realtor and selling my condo! So you and your prissy white bitch, Becky, better find another place to live. I'm coming back tomorrow to remove everything I brought in this bitch. When I come back, you and your bitch bet not be here, or I'mma have ya ass locked the fuck up for trespassing. As a matter of fact," I'm getting angrier every time I looked at Jayson. I thought to myself, and said fuck that, I yelled, "how about y'all get the fuck out now! I gotta cook my dinner, cause a bitch hungry and I'm tired." Pointing my finger in her face I said, "Ms. Sam, I suggest you grab all your belongings now, whatever don't belong to me will be trash!"

Jayson moved closer to me and said, "Mia, wait let's talk about this."

He tried to grab me by my waist as I walked passed his ass. I pushed him and raised my hand, as if I was gonna slap him again. He let me go and I told him, "hell, no! You should've been talked to me! Now this is what you get. I'm so over this and you, just get your shit, and ya bitch, and get the fuck out!"

Ole girl started getting her shit. She knew I was not playing no games. I'm watching her double check and make sure she got her shit. Jayson just standing there and he says, "Mia, I wanted us to be together, but you insisted on staying on the east coast." After taking a long pause he continues to say, "I was lonely, and I didn't expect to be with anyone long term, and we could never agree on what to do to make us work."

I started yelling, because he was full of shit. "Bullshit, Jayson! I tried several times to have a conversation about us and you kept putting it off." Shrugging my shoulders, I said, "it don't matter now, I'm done. Just get ya shit and get out!"

He was still standing there, so I figured he needed help. So I helped his ass out. I went into the bedroom and threw all his shit on the floor in the living room, shoes and all. I even threw a few things at his ass. I went into the kitchen and grabbed a few garbage bags and tossed them to his bitch and said, "bag that shit up, too!"

Like a good girl, the bitch was on her hands and knees bagging his shit. I sat on the bar stool at the kitchen counter, and I lit my blunt and looked at his ass and said, "what lies in the dark, becomes truth in the light, now get the fuck out!"

# Topaz

I haven't heard from Mia since she's been back in town, which is strange. I've been calling and

texting her without a response. I'mma call her one more time and leave a message. If she don't hit me back, me

and Jai going over to do a pop up. I know she hates that, but a bitch should've

answered my calls. It went to voicemail again, so I left a message and said, "Hey Mia, this is

Topaz, call me back and if I don't hear from you tonight, I'm coming thee fuck over there. You better answer the

fucking door."

Shit must have really went bad in LA. This was not like her to not respond to me or Jai. Later that morning

while I was at work, Jah called and said to meet him at the club. He wanted to take me to lunch. I was starving

too, since I didn't have breakfast. I'm gonna be in a meeting all morning, brainstorming for our next issue, and

having breakfast was not on the agenda. After reading my notes that I wrote prior to the meeting, I said, "Shane,

I read your piece and besides a few editing issues, I love it! I wanna use it as our cover story." I pointed towards

the graphics design door and said, "work with Drew for a cover photo. He has great ideas."

Jokingly I said, "I wanna know who is your source, because the details in it were unbelievable."

Waving his finger, no, He said, "now Ms. Topaz, you know I will not reveal my Source."

Acting disappointed I said, "humph, ok well in any case, great story. Whelp, that's all people, we'll pick up after

lunch."

As everyone was leaving, I picked up the phone and thought, let me try Mia one more time.

Damnit! Fucking voicemail again. Oh well, guess she'll have company tonight.

# __Mia__

Topaz called again, I'mma have to answer sooner or later. I whispered, "I'm tired." I turned to look into those beautiful brown eyes. With a smirk on his lips. He says,"well you shouldn't be such a freak, Ms. Me'asha."

Playfully rolling my eyes I said, "shut the fuck up, Tone. It's your fault anyway!"

He sat straight up like an arrow, holding his chest like he was clutching his pearls. "Oh, you blaming me now? If I can recall, you called me as soon as you landed."

With my cutest, sad puppy dog eyes I said, "that's because I missed you, and after I broke up with Jayson, all I wanted was to see your face. I love you."

"I love you more, Mia." He said. He kissed my lips so gently. It tasted like honey. He broke the kiss and said, "you never told me what happened out in LA. You looked stressed out when I picked you up. You must have really been jet lagged to leave your car in airport parking."

I started pulling my hair up in a ponytail, because I was ready for a shower. "Babe, I was exhausted, and thank you for having someone bring me my car. I really don't wanna talk about LA. Let's just say it's over, and now it's about us."

He looked me in my eyes and said, "if you having second thoughts, let me know now, so I can find a place to bury your ass."

Hahaha, I laughed out loud, and he kissed me on my neck, as my head tilted and said, "that's what I'm talking about!"

Looking confused I said, "what?"

His response was, "you! Laughing, that's what I love to hear."

He kissed me on my neck again and said, "I gotta run and handle some things for the grand opening in a few days. I'll call you tonight and see how you feeling. Check to see if you want me to come by. That is, if Topaz and Jai don't kill ya first."

Plopping my head in the pillow I started laughing and said, "I know right, but they'll be aight once I talk to them."

# Jai

Ever since me and Kaseem been back from Philly, it feels like we became closer. The love we

are experiencing is so fucking good! He had a nice surprise for me when we came back, keys to his now

finished house! I can't wait to show Mia and Topaz. We're meeting for lunch and baby, they gone be in shock!


**(lunch date)**


The waiter pulled my seat out for me to sit. While waiting for my sistas to arrive, I decided to

text Kaseem and let him know I was dropping off the groceries he asked for.

"Umm, excuse me miss, is this seat taken?"

Hearing this voice that sounded muffled, I look up and I rolled my eyes hard as hell.  I saw that it was Erica. I

stood up to greet her with a hug and kiss. I said, "Topaz, you play entirely too much, where is Mia?"

Pulling her chair out, she says, "I don't know, she left me a text saying she'll meet us here. You know she gotta

be fashionably late."

As I pour water into my glass, I just blurted out. "Kaseem gave me keys to his new place!"

Topaz stopped in her tracks and said, "get the fuck outta here, Jai!"

She was sitting there with her wine glass up to her face, like she about to tell me something, but she just stuck.

Here comes Mia, loud as usual. She bent over to kiss us on our cheeks and said,

"Hey ladies, and Topaz, why you looking like you got electrocuted?"

Before I can say anything, Topaz acting like she just got the best tea ever, like it wasn't about her

own sista. She says with excitement in her voice, "girl, Jai said that Kaseem gave her keys to his new place."

Now I got two zombies sitting here staring at me.

"Damn y'all, why you gotta be all extra and shit. We are in love and that's that! No more of me, being the topic of y'all tea, dammit!"

They looked at each other and smirked, and before you know it, they were singing, "*Awe shucks, Jai in love.*"

For the first time in a long time, I feel good about this relationship and I'm happy!

# **Topaz**

Here we go again, another work week. I feel real good about the article Shane wrote, this could

get us a whole new reader's group. Men talking about the game and how to get out and stay out. I tried to get

Jah to read it before it came out, but he was so not interested. He so busy worrying about Gems, the new

restaurant.

**(buzz)**

"Dee, get me Shane and tell him to meet me in conference room number 2 please." I have got to know how he

got this interview with one of the most notorious drug dealers in the city. I

remember this nigga when he was hustling dime bags of weed. I watched Shane walk down the

hallway, grinning from ear to ear. He was so proud of himself and so am I. I held the door open for him and

said, "Mr. Shane Powell, great article!" Closing the door behind him I continued to say, "So tell me, how you

do it?"

In his nonchalant manner, he said, "Do what?"

Sipping on my tea, I placed the new issue featuring his article on the table and said, "Shane, cut the bullshit, I'm

from the same hood where you got that interview, I know firsthand that you

just can't run up in there, talking about you a journalist tryna get a story. So you telling me everybody was like

'ok sure, what you wanna know?'"

He sat down at the far end of the conference table and said, "hahaha, Topaz, you know I will never tell my source or my tactics, but since you are the editor slash publisher, I'll tell you."

He got up and came closer.  He didn't want anyone to know, he spilling the tea. He leaned in and said, "I'm actually dating a relative who is close to Big Daddy."

In shock, I had to make sure that I'm hearing correctly and asked, "Big Daddy?" He confirmed by responding, "yes, Topaz, Big Daddy is the guy in the interview. I promised to not use his street name or his real name."

Yo, I'm buggin, the last I heard Big Daddy was doing a bid for like 15 years. I heard he got popped a few days after he called and left me that message. Wow, I wonder how he got out.  I said to Shane, "He was naming some heavy hitters in that interview. You better be careful not to get caught up in that street bullshit." Shit! Now that I know who it is, I'm kinda regretting publishing that article.

"I'm not worried, as long as he remains anonymous, I'm good!" Shane said.

After talking for an additional 10 minutes, I excused Shane and walked back to my office thinking, it's interesting that Jah's name wasn't mentioned. I'm glad it wasn't though. Now, I don't want Jah to read it. He may figure out who it is, and think I'm on some bullshit.

# Jah

I'm on the phone talking to my nigga, Jeff. He works at building codes and violations down at city hall. This nigga bullshitting and I'm mad as hell right now. Sipping on my yak, I said,

"Nigga, I ain't got time for your bullshit. I'm tryna open by next week. If I pay you, I expect what I paid for, nothing more, and nothing less. Get that fucking inspector over here today or we gone have a real motherfucking problem!"

I damn near broke the phone as I threw it across the room. These niggas think I'm playing, motherfuckers can't do shit right. All I needed to open is a clear inspection! What I don't need is the city to know about my un-zoned room, that I'm gonna be using for emergencies and for a stash spot. It seems like, I'm wasting my 20 g's on this nigga. I know he better do what I paid him to do or his momma shopping for a new black dress. Tryna calm myself, I looked at the pic of my queen sitting on my desk. I thought about dinner tonight with my queen, I'm missing her. She been doing a lot of work as of late, but that's because her issue came out. She been pressuring me to read the damn article, talking about it's something I'll like. She says it's talking about me, and how people like me, trying to get out and stay out the game. I didn't wanna read it, cause I'mma feel fucked up. I know damn well I'm not leaving the game. These businesses are to help me wash my money. Shit, the legit game is cool, but this hustle money is great, and Uncle Sam can't touch it. I really wanna do right by her and I know I told her I was changing, but how else would I get her to love me? It's just a little white lie. I picked up the advanced copy she left me, and shrugged my shoulders. I guess I'mma read this article, I don't want her to think that I'm not in support of her, and what she does. She's always supporting me, even if it is illegal and she don't know it. Walking pass the bouncer at The Strip, I nodded and heopened the door. He held it open until I exited the building. I'm going to get fresh and meet my queen!

# Kaseem

I'm chilling today and tryna get my family time in, I miss my boys. I've been running around the city, tryna make moves and spend as much time with Jai as possible. Especially since I'm tryna get this money from her. I know it's wrong, but I gotta do what I gotta do, to keep my family safe. I should have never got caught up in this bullshit. Sitting on the sofa in deep thought, and I realized how much I missed Trina. I sat up on the sofa looking around and I didn't see her, so I yelled, "Trina baby, come here, and sit next to daddy."

She came walking out the kitchen, looking so fine. Her hair was pulled up into one of those sloppy ponytails. I just wanted to fuck her right there on the floor. Then she started talking and said, "oh now, you daddy? Where was daddy last night, and the other nights, he supposed to be, daddy?"


This is the reason why my ass was never home. Every fucking time I tried to be a good dude and do some shit with her and the boys, she finds a way to fuck it up. Damn! I just looked at her and said, "damn Trina, why you always gotta be a fucking killjoy!?"

All I could do is look at her in amazement. She sat down across from me, crossed her legs, and said, "I'm not tryna kill your joy, but you walk around here like everything is ok. When everything's fucked up!"

I'm pissed now and I started yelling, "really Trina!? What's fucked up? Do you and the boys need or want for anything? Do you drive a fucking luxury car? Do you own your own home? It's not a 5 bedroom mansion, but it's better than that 1 bedroom flat I found ya ass in!"

As soon as the comment left my mouth I felt fucked up. Trina had a rough childhood, living in poverty and not knowing when and if she was gonna eat. Her dad died of a drug overdose and her momma was, and still is, a crackhead. I shouldn't have said that. The look on her face was a combination of disgust and hurt. Through the tears streaming down her face, she stood up and started walking towards me. She pointed her finger in my face and screamed, "fuck you, Kas! I didn't sign up to have kids with a man who only wanted to run the streets all fucking day and night. You probably fucking bitches, too. Crackhead bitches at that!"

Yo I swear, it took everything in me not to say, you right, including ya momma! Who gives thee best head on the block, but I thought that would have been a little too much. I stood up to match her stance and I grab her hands. I simply replied, "Trina, I know I haven't been doing my husband and Father duties as of late, but I promise you, I'm working on getting out for real this time." I sat down again, hoping that shit could calm down and she sat on the other couch,

like she didn't wanna be around me. So I got up and sat on the couch next to her. I held her hand and continued to say, "I just wanna chill out with my wife and boys without thinking about the street life, just for today please. The last thing I wanna do is argue with you. I love you, and I promised I would take care of you and my sons and that's what I'm tryna do. Can we please at least pretend? Just for today? Let's pretend everything is normal."

I looked at her with sincere pleading eyes, waiting for a response. She just looking at me and she said nothing. Instead she just kissed me and called the boys in, so we could watch a movie together. I love this woman, and I feel bad for what I'm doing. It's all a part of the game of life.

# __Anthony__

## Tone

This grand opening for Gems is going to be the bomb dot com. I'm so glad that me and Jah decided to go legit. I wanna live right and I wanna live right, with Mia. We could be the power couple we are destined to be. Let Jah tell it though, him and Topaz are the truth. I gotta reach out to my baby, and see how things coming along with her part.

**(phone ringing)**

The sound of her voice always makes me turn into mush. When she answered, I said,

"hey, sweet momma."

She loves it when I call her that. She replied in her innocent voice.

"Hey daddy, what's up?"

"Nothing, just thinking about you and wondering how things are coming, with the hiring of your staff and the menu."

I like to get the business out the way. Then we can get all lovey dovey and shit. She even switched up real quick, she put on her business voice and said, :Everything is falling in place. I have hired all of my staff and I've ordered all the supplies. Even though this one vendor I've been working with for years, is giving me a little trouble. Talking about, he don't know if he wanna extend my contract for *this* restaurant."

Now my ears are tweaking. I put the chair in the upright position. Did she say somebody not working with her?

"What he mean by, '*this restaurant* ?'" I said. I already know why, I just needed to hear it before I go put in this work. I know I'm supposed to be handling things the legit way, however, one thing I'm not doing is, I'm not letting anybody come between my money and business. Nope, I'm not having it.

She continued to say, "He said, he's not working with hustlers and I shouldn't either. I didn't even go on to explain, I just said 'fuck it!' You know ya girl got connects, I don't really need him. It was just easier since we've done business together in the past."

Shid, I'm thinking too late! Shouldn't have told me, now I'mma have to check this nigga. So next time he come across my baby, he knows what time it is. I just said, "Ok baby, as long as you got it under control. If you need help, let me know." She don't need to know everything and I continued on saying, "I don't know much about what you doing and shit, but I'll help you in every way I can. Even if I gotta resort to my old ways of checking a motherfucker!"

I laughed at what I said, but I'm serious as hell.

"Baby, I'm good. How's things on your end?" She said.

"It's all good baby, the investors like the location and most importantly, they love the turnaround numbers. Anything where they make a huge profit on their investment, they're happy. We gonna do more business together as well, so things over here looking real good." I said. I'm really excited about this new venture. I'm really looking forward to doing things right and telling the police, fuck you! I ended the convo so I could relax, and she can do what it is she do. Exhaling my cigar smoke, I was feeling more relaxed and I said, "Well baby, get back to work and I'll see you later. Maybe you can come by my house tonight."

She don't like coming in the hood where I live. It's really not that bad, I'd rather live in the hood where I know what I'm getting, instead of the suburbs, where them white motherfuckers chop you up and eat ya ass for dinner. Fuck that! Give me a hungry crackhead any day, I know how to handle that motherfucker.

"Ok daddy, I love you," she said, in her sweet voice.

# Grand Opening

# Topaz

Tonight is a big night! Not only is my man having his grand opening, but my sissy, Mia, is showing off her culinary arts skills. I'm so proud of both of them. I'm especially proud of Jah, for setting his goals and accomplishing them the right way! Jah should be on his way. We are leaving a little late to meet up with Mia and Tone. I'm thinking about, how we came from the hood and became successful people, despite our rough childhood, which was filled with drugs and violence. It's a very satisfying feeling and, I'm so very proud of all of us. I hate when people say that nothing good come from the hood. We are living proof that it does and I can't wait to show off. Why is he ringing that doorbell like he done lost his mind. I yelled and said, "one minute!" Ok, that's my bae. I took one last look before I opened the door, and I'm looking good. Jai styled me and I love this red mini dress. The way the back is cut out, Omg, it's fire. I damn near ran to the door. I opened it with a big smile and said, "Hey, daddy!"

This nigga sharper than a tact! With his black tux and red bow tie. He walked in looking at me from head to toe, grinning. He was showing them bright white teeth and he said, "damn baby, that dress fitting you right!"

I gave him a little preview by spinning around, so he can get a 360 view, I'm thinking yeah, I know! Laughing to myself I said, "Thanks, babe."

Shit I'm looking at this nigga with eyes full of lust! He broke my thoughts by saying, "girl, we look so good together." He kissed me and asked, "you ready?"

Hell yeah! But going out ain't on my mind. This nigga really matching my fly! It's sexy as hell. I tried to sound real seductive when I said, "yes baby, I'm ready."

# Kaseem

"Trina, I'm telling you, I'm not doing shit." I'm trying to get her to chill out!

"Yeah right, Kas! So you telling me that, the bitch callin ya phone every morning is ya connect?"

Shit, I had to tell her something, I rather her think I'm hustling instead of cheating. I'm damn near begging her to believe this bullshit. "Baby listen, I got ole girl to be my overnight lookout and because things are hot, I make her call me every morning. She lets me know how business is doing before the shift change. I gotta stay a step ahead, if I'm tryna get out." She looked at me with her lips twisted. I knew she didn't believe me, Trina would rather hear a lie anyway. She really gonna be mad once I tell her I have a business meeting tonight. I continued to say,"Babe, we'll talk more about this when I get home." She snapped her head around so quick, I put my mild out, cause I didn't know what was next. "Fuck you mean, when you get back!? Let me guess, another business meeting?" She said. I tried to respond, but she threw her hands up to keep from saying anything. She walked out and continued to say, "shut the fuck up, Kas and just get the fuck outta my face!"

I lit my mild and put my shoes on and left. Soon as I pulled out the driveway, she texting me and cussing me out as usual. "Fuck!" I screamed loud as hell out of frustration. I know Jai cussing me out too, she been blowing my phone up.

# Jai

Here we go again, I thought we were over this little hump. I see that he's putting more effort into us, but it's times like this, that makes me wonder. I've been calling Kaseem for over an hour and still no answer. Next, I'mma go over to his house, an hour later, this nigga ringing my fucking doorbell and I hauled ass to the door, ready to cuss his ass out! Soon as I opened it, I lit into his ass. "Kaseem, I've been calling you for hours!" I exaggerated the time, but so the fuck what. Not waiting for a response I said, "did you forget we going to Gems tonight?"

He looked like he wasn't paying my ass any mind and in a smart ass tone he said,

"clearly, I didn't forget, I'm here, ain't I?"

I looked at his ass like he bumped his head.

"I don't know what's going on with you, but whatever it is, don't take it out on me!" I said.

I just grabbed my keys and my purse and walked passed his ass. He knew I was pissed!

# Mia

I'm so excited about tonight! I just got off the phone with the prep and line cooks and they ready,

they're just waiting on me. Coming out the bathroom, I asked Tone, "babe, you ready?"

I looked at him with admiration. I was very proud of him and grateful he brought me along for the ride.

He looked me in my eyes and nervously said, "as ready as I'll ever be."

While helping him adjust his tie, he stopped and looked me in my eyes and sweetly said,

"I love you, Ms. Meisha Lawson!"

Holding back my tears, I moved in closer to his face, and looked him in those brown eyes and kissed him just as

gently, saying, "I love you more, baby." He looked like he was tearing up, too! He grabbed my hand and said,

"let's go, Ms. Lady, and take over brick city!"


# Topaz

Damn, the parking lot full as hell. Glad we had the bouncer rope off two parking spaces. Jah came around to

open my door, like the true gentleman he is. As I stepped out, he kissed me and said, "I love you."

In awe of him, I blushed and was grinning from ear to ear. I replied, "I love you, too."

Mia and Tone pulled up and I'm loving how Jai styled her. She had on a beautiful white pants suit and her hair

pulled up in a perfect bun. Perfect for her being in the kitchen for long periods of time. As they approached us, I

looked at her from head to toe and said, "Damn Mia, you cooking or are you cooking!

I'm so proud of you guys!" I said, still holding back my tears.

Mia said, "thanks, Topaz. Jai did her thing, didn't she?"

"Yes, she did." I said.

I saw Jai pull into the parking lot, then Mia turned and looked at me and said, "damn, Tone! Why y'all ain't get parking for Jai?"

I'm looking at Jah's face like, yeah why not? After looking at the expression on my face, Tone quickly spoke and said, "it wasn't intentional, I just figured it was a better look for just the owners and their wives."

Jah tried to make it right by interrupting Tone. "No worries, we gonna wait so we can all go in together." He better had said something, because he saw the look of disappointment on my face. Jai and Kaseem started walking towards us, and she was beautiful! That nude dress is banging! Hugging all her curves. Kaseem looked nice in his blue suit too, but I just don't like him! I'mma chill though, cause Jai loves him. When she reached us, Jai gave everyone a hug and said,

"Hey, guys and ladies, y'all lookin real nice."

Jai looks so happy and I'm happy for her. I looked at myself like I needed a reminder and said,

"Hey sissy, why thank you. You gotta meet my stylist."

Mia chuckled at my little funny. The men exchanged handshakes and we proceeded inside. As I walked in, I was amazed. I knew it would be nice, but it's better than I thought. As I looked around, I said, "Oh, Jah and Tone, this place is beautiful!" Looking around at the decor, you can tell Mia had her woman's touch imprinted here. Tone has pride written all over his face, as he said to me, "thanks Topaz, your man came through and now we both can live, Finally!"

We were escorted to our circular table in the center of the restaurant. The waiter brought over a bottle of champagne and we made a toast! Before I could ask, Jai beat me to it and asked,

"So Mia, are you sitting with us, or are you in the kitchen tonight?"

Mia sipped her champagne before answering and said, "Jai, I'mma be out here. I made sure everything is good, and from what I see, everybody looks happy."

Tone looked at Mia like he really loves her. You can see the love, he grabbed the back of her neck and said,

"my baby got it under control, and I'm sure everything will be good."

I'm looking around and I notice we have no menus. So I asked, "where's the menu"?

Jah chuckled and said, "Topaz, we have menus, babe, but Mia decided to prepare us a variety of samples."

I looked at her for clarification and she responded, "yes, I prepared everybody's favorite and a few samples of the menu items. Kaseem, I didn't know what you liked, so I prepared a steak for you. Everybody loves a good steak."

He was acting like he preoccupied with something else. Jai looked at him and he spoke,

"Steak is fine, thank you."

I couldn't get over how nice it really looked in here and I said, "the restaurant is really nice. You brothers doing the damn thing."

Jah sipped his champagne and he looked like he's not beat for Kas. Jah tried to get Kaseem's attention by saying, "well Kaseem, once you get your own business up and running, maybe we can do some things."

As much as I love Jah, that sounded so fake. I just kept the convo moving along. We had a great dinner and the opening was really nice. They had a huge turn out! I can't wait to get home though.

# Topaz

I don't have time to bullshit today. I'm walking in the office today focused. I zoomed by Dee's desk barking orders and shit, "Dee, bring my coffee to conference room 2, and grab the folders off my desk, we have a busy day today!" I can feel his eyes on the back of my head and he quickly said, "well good morning, to you too, Ms. Topaz."

I stopped and turned around with my glasses pulled down to the tip of my nose and said, "good morning, Miss Dee. "He loves it when I call him *Miss.* With his smart mouth he said, "better, now I'll meet you in room 2." Wondering what is taking Dee so long to get here, I looked down the hall and why is Dee damn near running down here? I met him halfway and ask, "Dee, what's wrong? Why you look scared?" He was so flustered that, he was damn near outta breath.

"Topaz, girl the police down the hall locking up Shane!" He said.

"What? Why?" I said.

"I don't know but he got cuffs on."

I ran down the hall to check it out. "Excuse me officer, but what's the problem?" Two white cops looked like they caught the big fish. They were nasty too! One officer said, "Miss, he's being arrested for obstruction of justice. In other words, failure to cooperate with NPD."

I'm in shock, Shane's just standing there and he doesn't even look scared. I asked, "Shane, are you ok?"

He stood tall and spoke loud and clear. "I'm fine Ms. Topaz, just like I told you, I'm never giving up my source, they got me fucked up."

Well alright then. I bet they wanna know who he know and how he got that story. Before they shoved him in the elevator, I yelled, "I'll call Les!"

I grabbed my coffee and headed to my office. "Dee, get me Lester Brown." He's the company's attorney. Dee looks at me serious as a heart attack, and asked, "ok, you want me to sit in on this for note taking?" I gave his ass that raised eyebrow like, really bitch? "No thanks nosey, just make the call."

# Tone

1st Official day at Gems and I can't wait to start making that money. I got the best chef in New Jersey. My baby, who should already be there taking inventory. I grabbed my keys and my phone and as soon as I closed my door, the phone rings. "Hello, hello? Who's this?" Nobody saying shit, as soon as I get ready to hang up, I hear someone say, "Tone, this Shawn from 19th Ave., Big got locked up!"

I turned around and went back in the house and said, "Fuck you mean, he got locked up! For what?" I couldn't believe what I was hearing.

Shawn said, "I don't know, the boys came through and snatched him up."

The boys just coming through? That doesn't sound right, especially since Big Daddy just came back from Virginia. "What was Big doing on the block anyway?" I asked.

"He was passing through and got out to holla at us!"

I looked around and grabbed my trap phone and left. As I'm walking to my truck I tell Shawn,

"aight, you and the rest of y'all meet me at Savoy's tonight at 10 and dress the part nigga. No white tee's and boots. Tell them niggas to dress like they going out."

I gotta call Jah and tell him to meet me at Savoy's tonight. Once I get in my truck, I tell Siri to call Jah.

# Jai

I have to prepare my things for my trip to Atlanta. It's a big fashion show out there and I gotta be apart of it. As I'm searching for this dress, I hear my assistant Tasha talking to someone.

"Thank you, sir. I'll sign for them."

I quickly put the hanger back and went out to see who she was talking to. I said, "Tash, who was that? Oh never mind, I see somebody has a boyfriend, huh? You didn't tell me about this one, honey." I pulled up the little foot stool and sat down to get the tea.

Tasha started laughing and said, "girl, I don't know about no boyfriend, but you sure got somebody who likes you, these are yours!"

I sat there looking confused as hell, I was not expecting that. I covered my mouth and spoke through my hand and said, "what? For real, Tash?" I grabbed them out of Tasha's hand and said, "oh, these are beautiful, and I know who they from, too." A big smile came across my face as I thought about Kaseem, and how much he thought about me and him lately.

Tasha brought me a vase and said, "well Jai, you must be putting it on a brother, got the nigga sending you flowers and shit, he got any brothers?"

I laughed at that thought in my head, I would never hook her up with anyone I know. Won't be blaming me for hooking you up with a girl from around the way. Don't get me wrong, I love Tash. She cool as hell, just not ready for the caliber of men I know, not yet anyway. We all were the same way back in the day and look at us now. I grabbed my flowers and took them to my office and I called Kaseem. Asusual he never answers. I don't know why every time I call this man he never answers, but always calls me back at his convenience. I'm trying not to ruin the moment with my way of thinking, but dammit man. Tasha knocked on the door and then poked her head in and said, "Jai, you have a call on line 2."

Shaking my head, all I could think to myself was I knew it, must be Kaseem.

"Hello, this is Jai."

"Hey, Jaiden." She said.

I sat up straight, because I didn't recognize the voice and she called me by full name. Confused I said, "hello, may I ask who's speaking?" Staring at my desk waiting and I repeat, "Hello?"

Just when I was about to hang up, I heard her saying, "Hello suga, this ya Aunt Mae."

I sat down grinning, I love my aunt Mae. I was happy to hear from her. With excitement in my voice I said, "Hey, auntie what's up? How are you!?"

My auntie is my dad's sister and still lives in the pj's. She's like the hood mother down there, everybody loves her. She got some bad ass kids though. They all in a gang and hustle. They're into everything you can imagine, I love them though. She started talking clear now that she knows it's me. Just as loud and ghetto as ever she says, "I'm good honey, hanging in there. Listen, I'm calling to ask you something."

I wonder how much she needed now. As much as I love her, she only calls when she needs something. I do it anyway, because she's my auntie, and helped raised me too. After a sigh, I asked, "what's that, auntie?" In her sweetest country voice she says, "I wanna give Jr. a birthday party, but I wanna have it somewhere real nice though. You think you can help me out, by giving me a little extra money to have it somewhere nice?"

Now, I love my little cousin Jr. but he into the streets heavy, and I really don't wanna be a part of anything for Jr., but it's auntie so I said, "Ok auntie, I'll be there today and we can talk about what's what."

Well, I guess we'll be going to the hood ball of the year. Let me call Topaz and Mia. Ain't no way I'm attending this alone.

# Jah

I walked into The Strip tonight feeling a little apprehensive. I didn't want to ruin the atmosphere in there, but having a meeting with the soldiers is critical. I passed through trying to make it to my office, but people keep stopping me and wanting to talk. I talked to a few, shook a few hands, but I kept it pushing for the most part. I walked into a room full of gangsters, looking like they going to a funeral. These niggas are straight street niggas. Tone got up and greeted me with a hug and a dap and said, "what's good with it, Jah?"

"I can't call it my nigga, I'm tryna figure out how Big got knocked off!"

I walked over to my desk and pulled out my dutch and give it to Tone to light and said, "Somebody gotta know something. No way in hell less than 12 hours of Big being back in town, he gets knocked off. According to the lawyers, they got him on trafficking drugs, parole violation, and weapons possession. Somebody snitched on him!"

I'm tryna pay attention to everybody's body language, but I don't see any movement. Tone passed me the blunt and I let him say what he wanted. He started walking around in circles like he playing duck duck goose and shit. He stopped suddenly and said, "Now listen, if y'all know who the rat is, I suggest you say it now, cause later if we find out you knew, but didn't say shit. Ya family going shopping for a casket, and if you don't know, find out! Put your ear to the street and find out who this rat bastard is."

I had to let them know that we not playing no games. I passed the blunt back to Tone. These niggas can't smoke with us. They not on our level and that's what they better know. I simply said in a calm tone, "listen, on some real shit, it really don't matter if y'all don't say shit, cause when that paperwork come out, everything we gonna need to know, will be there in black and white."

Some looked a little confused as I walked over to my desk and pulled out a bottle and a glass. Poured myself a shot, took it back, and continued what I was saying, "In case some of y'all don't know, that's the paperwork with the whole case basically laid out. From witnesses, to locations of all activities, and all the snitches!"

Tone interrupted and said, "so basically, it's the whole investigation in print. Oh, and when we get that paperwork, y'all gonna have to put in that work."

Meaning, get rid of the snitches before court. I told them niggas I'll be in touch with them and they better get me some info I can use. After they left, Tone and I sat back and talked about this Big situation. Tone looked as confused as I felt.

"Yo Jah, who the fuck would wanna take us out? When we trying to get out?"

"I don't know man, but whoever it is, is a damn fool. It seems like the more we try to get out, the more it just keeps sucking us in." I said.

Tone got up to go and make himself a drink. While walking to the bar he said, "Jah, whatever we do, we can't get into no war with none of these niggas. We tryna exit and fucking with these niggas, we gon' always be looking behind us."

Smoking my blunt, all I could do was agree to not disagree. The gangster in me wants war and don't wanna leave the life. A part of me knows, it's not a good look on what I'm trying do and truthfully, I know it's either death by murder or jail, neither of which I want. I have a lady that I love now and someday I wanna marry and have babies with. It's something about this Big issue that's not sitting with me too well. I feel like I need to get to the bottom of this and then I'll be out. I walked over to where Tone was standing, and said, "Tone, listen I think whoever it is knows we want out, but knows we still have ties in the streets. So they

trying to shut down the whole operation. They knew Big getting knocked would stop all movement. This is what they want, fuck them! I'mma call Hak and get some shit from him and get Big out. They want a quarter of a million for his bail. You know we can't do cash. The feds would be all on us." I saw Tone looking at me weird as hell like, he knows what's next. I just take a couple of quick pulls of my blunt and just shoot straight from the hip and say, "we gonna use the restaurant as collateral, but that means, we need Mia's signature too, because she on the deed." He is not going to like this, but we gotta do, what we gotta do. Tone walked away from me and sat down, looking stressed the fuck out.

"Jah, I really don't wanna do that! I would have to tell her what for and she not gonna like

this shit at all!"

"I know, but you'll figure it out. No worries, we not gonna lose the business, make sure you really reiterate that

to her." I said.

Messing with her reputation and our money, is not something I'm into, so that won't happen. Tone was nervous as hell, I could hear it in his voice. He agreed anyway and said, "aight man, but I'm telling you, this don't look

good at all my friend, not at all."

# Mia

There is no way in hell that I'm telling Topaz or Jai, that I signed my part of the restaurant over to a damn bank for collateral for a damn bail, especially for Big Daddy, they would have a fit. At first, I didn't wanna do it. Tone said that he would never put me in a situation where I would lose so much money and we'll get it back with no worries. I trust him and I know he wouldn't put me in any bullshit. It's just paperwork. Jai called me the other day and asked if Tone and I would go to Jr.'s party with her, and we told her yeah. I think Topaz is going too, which I'm surprised. She got a lot going on at her job, people getting locked up and shit. It's crazy. I can't wait to see my girls again; it seems like it's beenforever. We all been busy with our love lives and work.

**(Phone ringing)**

"Hello, this is Topaz."

"Hey sistaaaaa! I miss you!" After I got myself together, I sat back down and lit me a cigarette. A habit I just picked up. Topaz sounded happy too.

"I miss you too, girl! I can't wait to see you tonight. You going to Jr's party, right?"

I should fuck with her since she so excited, so I said, "no, we not going tonight. We just gonna stay in, cause we be so busy with work, plus I'm tryna run an additional 2 restaurants. It's tiring, Tee." I pushed the mute button so I could laugh out loud. I can tell she not liking what I was saying. All I heard was deep breathing. I can imagine her eyebrows frowning up. After a very deep breath, Topaz said, "ok Mia, as much as I don't like it, I have to respect it. You are doing a lot. I just wished you were there, but no worries, maybe we can have lunch one-day next week."

I know this bitch is lying, I know her ass is mad. I started laughing out loud and I said, "sike, Tee we coming, you know damn well I'm not missing an opportunity to turn the fuck up with my sistas."

"I knew ya ass was lying bitch, you love to fucking party. Stop fucking playing, cause you know if our asses don't show up, we will never hear the end of it."

I laid the cigarette down and told Tee I would call her back. I saw Tone pulling up. I got up to open the door and I waited in the doorway until he got out. Tone is looking more and more like Derek Luke, the actor. He's so fine, with that beautiful brown skin, and nice plump lips. He walked right passed me, no kiss no nothing. Right away I asked, "baby, what's wrong?" I sat on the couch and watched him walk to the kitchen for a beer. I watched him pace back and forth. I begged him to tell me what's wrong.

"Baby? Please! What's wrong?"

"They killed Shawn!" He whispered.

I don't know who Shawn is. It must be someone close to him. This man was in the house crying. I hugged him tight as I could and said, "aww baby, I'm sorry to hear that." What else am I to say? I didn't know him. I just asked, "what happened? Are you ok?"

He got up, walked towards the bedroom and angrily he screamed at me, "Am I ok? Do I look ok, Mia? What kinda dumb ass question is that to ask me?!"

As much as I wanted to curse his ass out, I knew that he was hurting. So I'mma let him get that for right now. I walked over to him and grabbed his face. I looked into his eyes and sincerely said, "baby, I'm sorry. Let me make you something to eat, you hungry?"

I always suggest food for every situation. Shit, food always makes me feel better. I walked toward the Kitchen, but he stopped me and said, "no! I don't want no fucking food!"

He must have saw the hurt in my eyes. He stopped and said, "I'm sorry for yelling at you, come here, baby."

As I walked towards him, all I saw was lust in his eyes, and I think I'm about to get that angry sex. The closer I get to him, the more wet my panties become. I want him to ravish me like an animal. Once I got in his face, he kissed me so hard, I jumped on him with my legs wrapped around his waist. With his hands cuffing my booty, I'm kissing his neck and he biting on mines. The shit hurt so good! He carried me to my bedroom and placed me on the bed. My legs still wrapped around his waist, he grabbed both my thighs and positioned my legs up. He slipped off my panties with his teeth and ate my pussy like a starving caveman. My legs started shaking and I was trying to catch my breath. I closed my eyes and stopped fighting the urge, and the next thing I know, everything went black! I was out for about 3 minutes. Tone thought I was just recouping from that orgasm. I sounded out of breath, but I managed to say, "damn baby, a bitch almost died." Holding my legs together so they could stop trembling, Tone started

laughing and said, "Mia, I done ate that pus many times? What happened?" He was laughing uncontrollably and I'm still tryna catch my breath.

"I don't know, babe, but whatever that mouth was doing, got the job done!"


Glad he's feeling better, hopefully we can continue in the spirit of feeling good. I eased in my next statement by stroking his dick and saying, "babe, Jai invited us to her cousin Jr.'s birthday party. You wanna go?"

I'm licking my lips and wanting him to say yes. He moaned, cause that stroke felt good. He said,

"not really, but if you wanna go, I'll go."

I knew he would do anything for me. I jumped up and ran in the bathroom and guess who followed me holding that monster dick? I invited him in with me and said, "come here, daddy, let me give that monster a kiss.

# Jai

Kaseem better not disappoint me tonight. Tonight, he meets my family and I ain't for his shit. I guess I'll give him the benefit of doubt, lately he's been making me and us a priority. Although he's flying in from Atlanta, he said he'll be there.

**(Phone ringing)**

Please don't be bad news, I put my grinder down and dreaded the phone ringing. I answered and a familiar voice responded, "what's good wit it, cousin?!"

I started smiling instantly! It was my cousin Jr.

"Hey Jr., you ready for tonight!?"

I picked up my weed and started rolling. He sounded happy. "Yeah, I'm ready, hope you got some bad bitches for me," he said.

"You always asking me for bitches. No I don't, Jr." I laughed after I said that. He hates the name Jr.

"Aye, what I tell you about that. Listen though, I'll be there around 10," he said.

Auntie gon' be mad about that. She hates waiting. I quickly reminded him and said

"Now Jr., you know auntie wants you there by 9. Why I got to be the one who knows you gone be late?"

"Well shit, act like you don't know, Jai. I just need you to leave me a key to ya spot," he said.

I looked at the phone like, nigga who? I said, "hell no! For what?" I started pulling on my blunt cause I thought I was hearing shit. Here he go with some bullshit ass story and he said,

"Since I moved to Philly, when I come home mommy house ain't where I should be. I gotta be low-key.Can't let motherfuckers know where I sleep. Nobody in the hood knows where you stay."

"Ok Jr., but no bullshit in my house, nothing! Unless you bringing me some weed."

Jr knows that I know, he brings work to the city. I don't want the shit in my house. He started laughing. "Aight, chill cuz, I'm only coming to turn the fuck up with my peoples. I got you on the weed. Relax."

Relax my ass. Last time he was just chilling, the nigga got shot sitting on my auntie stoop. That's why his ass in fucking Philly! I'mma trust this fool.

"Aight Jr., I'mma leave the key in my mailbox. What am I supposed to say to auntie, when she looking at my ass wondering where yo ass is?"

"Jai, just say you don't know," he said.

"Whatever nigga, do what you gotta do and make the damn party that I paid for, nigga!"

"Chill, ma, I'mma be there. I'll see you later and thanks for letting me squat at ya crib."

# Jah

I was sitting in my office when I got the call about Shawn. What the fuck is going on? First Big gets knocked off and can't nobody find the product, and now Shawn, my number two man gets popped! I know damn well, somebody tryna get me cased up, shutdown, or killed. Either way, whoever is responsible, has it out for me and Tone. We better find out who it is before it's too late. Let me call my mans to see who on shift right now. My man answered his phone fast as hell. He knows that when he see my number, it's a motherfucking problem. I said,

"Aye Jon Jon, who trapping on 9th Ave and south 12th Street?" That's where Shawn got popped at. "I don't know, Jah. I think it was that little nigga, Cory." I'm thinking that little nigga knows something. No bullshit, I need to see that little nigga. I told Jon Jon to bring his ass to me, ASAP!

# Kaseem

Jai thinks I'm in Atlanta, but I'm home, chilling with my family. Trina been really bugging lately, so I set it up for my boy, Cory, to call me and say anything. That will be my excuse to leave and attend this party Jai wants me to go to. I gotta meet Hak tonight, too. I figured if, Cory calls me at 8, I can meet Hak at 9:30 like he insisted. I'm glad I don't have to drive to Philly and drop him this money. He in town on some personal shit and he said he'll call me with the location to meet him. I don't have all his money though. I'm looking at the time and I figured I better at least eat with them. "Trina baby, you wanna order some pizza for the boys and we go out for dinner?"

I'm looking at my beautiful brown skin cutie, looking like a short Kenya Moore from Atlanta Housewives.

Next thing I knew; my fantasy was blown. She said, "who gonna watch the boys? Why don't we all go out to eat?"

I took a deep breath and tried not to sound like an asshole and I said, "baby, I just wanted it to be us, we can call ya sister to come babysit. She'll do it if I pay her."

I know she ain't goin for that. The last time Shannon babysat for us, she had her friends over and they were sitting on the porch smoking weed. She responded the way I expected her to.

"You know my mother said she wasn't allowed over here to babysit anymore."

I overheard her mother say once before that, she thought Shannon got the weed out of my house!

Says the crackhead! That couldn't be further from the truth. I would never bring any drugs to my

house with my family. People will judge you, whether you doing good or bad. She has already labeled me as the

bad boy.

Annoyed I said, "Ok, so what you wanna do? But yelling at the boys all night in a restaurant is not what I call

US time. We'll just order take out and watch a movie."

Another boring ass night, but this what she likes so it's whatever. Looking for my phone and it must be in the

room. I yelled and said, "Trina, can you bring me my phone out the room, it's on the charger."

Time to text Cory and Hak. Two hours later, with my belly full and the kids asleep, Trina sucked my dick so

good, I almost went to sleep! Until my phone rang.

I answered, "Hello." Looking at Trina as she started to fall asleep.

"Yo, this Cory, you good?"

Trying to make it sound like it's an emergency, I say, "Hey John, what's up?"

Cory thinks this shit funny and says, "John? Really nigga, listen Jah had one of his goons come scoop me up off

the block." Oh shit! I sat straight up, cause this really is an emergency. I tried to whisper and said, "What? For

what?" Trying not to panic, I went into the den so Trina wouldn't hear me.

Cory said, "he asked what happened when Shawn got popped, and who was out there."

Holding my head in disbelief, I'm tryna think how the fuck he knew to ask Cory, specifically. Looking out the

window because I'm paranoid and I said, "I hope you didn't say shit nigga, I paid you 5 grand to keep your

mouth shut and your eyes open." Pouring me a drink and my phone started beeping, I got the text from Hak. I

drank a shot real quick andsaid, "aight well, keep doing what I paid you to do. Keep me posted if anybody else

questions you. I'll be in touch."

I didn't even look at Hak's text, I just got dressed and told Trina I had an office emergency. She was half sleep,

so no arguments. I grabbed my bag out the garage and got in the car. Once I got in, I realized I didn't know

where I'm going. I looked at the text and realized Hak texted me Jai's address! Looking in my rearview mirror like, this is some sort of setup.  What the fuck is going on here? Let me call Jai. she answered, "Hello, this is Jai."

I pulled over, cause I'm not moving till I fully understand what's going on.

In a calm voice I said, "hey baby, where are you?" She sounded normal to me.

"Hey babe, I'm on my way to the party, where are you?" She said.

The fuck! I'm confused as hell now; I'm thinking it's a setup. Damn, is Jai tryna set me up? Did she find out about Trina? I answered and said,

"I'm actually home, I took an earlier flight to be there for you tonight. I know how important it is that I meet the family."

All I hear is a bunch of noise in the background. I asked her, "baby, did you hear me? What's going on?"

I heard her say, "Oh shit!" I started panicking and shit and I start yelling.  "Baby, what?"

"Damn baby, it's a bad accident on 280, the shit look crazy, so where are you?"

Feeling relieved I said, "I'm home on my way to meet you."

I didn't even feel like repeating myself, I'm caught up in why the fuck Hak text me her address. She probably fucking that nigga too. She didn't sound as excited as I thought she would.

"Aww, that's good baby. I can't wait for you to meet my family. Call me when you outside, I'll be there in about 7 minutes."


Ok, now I don't know if I should go over there or not. If I don't go, then Hak will kill my ass and if I do go, he still might kill my ass. Sitting here with my hazard lights on contemplating. I sat up and said fuck that, I'm not going, I'll meet him somewhere else.


**(phone ringing)**


Hak sounded like he was just sitting on a throne somewhere, his voice deeply said,

"What's good with it?"

I'm trying to sound like I have something important to handle. I replied, "What's good wit it, my nigga? Listen, I'm at the hospital with my son. He fell off his bike and broke his arm. I'm waiting for it to get casted up, how about we meet tomorrow at Slicks around 9pm?"

I used my son as an excuse, Lord forgive me, but something just ain't sitting right with me, and meeting this nigga at Jai's house.

Hak agreed and said, "aight nigga, you better not be trying to play me the fuck out. You know that shit will cost you ya life, my nigga."

I pulled out into traffic to meet Jai. Feeling a little better I said, "no bullshit, my dude, I'mma holla at you tomorrow though." Aight, this gives me time to get Cory and them to suit up, just in case this an ambush.

# Topaz

I'm twisting my hair in an up do cause I don't wanna sweat my shit out. I love hood parties though. It takes me back to where I'm from. Jai said it's not a hood party, but if everybody at the motherfucker from the hood, then it's a hood party. Jah seemed a little preoccupied to pay my ass any attention. Tryna get him outta his little funk I say, "Jah, suga dumpling what's wrong, baby? You haven't said 2 words to me since you got here."

I'm looking at him through the mirror and all I see is a frown on his face.

He says with a shaky voice, "babe I'm good, I'm just upset about my boy getting popped the other day. He was my mans for real, for real and I'mma miss that nigga."

I feel bad for Jah, but at the same time grateful that it's not him. I turned around to face him and I say "babe, I know it's hard, I would be lost if something happened to my sistas."

I pulled the dresser drawer out and lit the blunt I had in there, and passed it to Jah and said,

"Here baby, this will make you feel a little better." I watched him take long pulls of that blunt and even though he was feeling sad right now, I couldn't help but think about how sexy his ass looked smoking. His hair is growing nicely too, them dreads is sexy as fuck on him. He passed it back to me and I just took one pull and passed it, I don't wanna be too high at the hood party. Gotta keep my eyes and ears open, you never know what could pop off.

He put the blunt out and said, "Topaz, I'm gonna jump in the shower real quick and I could use someone to wash my back, if you don't mind."

Mind? Hell no! I started looking for my head scarf and took off my tee shirt and followed him in. Wash his back? Yeah right! I'mma wash something alright. I looked at him up and down and said, "ok babe, go ahead I'm coming."

# Partytime

## Jai

The Tucker Center looks nice when it's decorated. I see a bunch of people I grew up with and I also see my

favorite auntie in the whole wide world. "Hey, auntie." I kneeled down to kiss her forehead.

She responded in her country ass accent and said, "hey sweetie, thank you so much for your help and planning

this for Jr., I can't wait till he gets here."

She was looking around the center and said, "why that boy always gotta be late for shit?"

I just laughed at her comment and excused myself. My phone is vibrating and it's a text from Kaseem telling

me he's outside. I put my drink down and walked very carefully, I was trying to be cute with these shoes. When

I got outside, he was standing right at the door. I smiled and said,

"Hey love, you lookin real handsome tonight."

I leaned in for a kiss, but it was half ass on his part. He was looking around like he was looking for someone

and said, "thanks babe, you look nice, too. How's the party going so far?"

He acted like he was just making small talk with his boys. I looked puzzled and said,

"The party is going to be lit. It's already crowded and people are in there dancing. You know the hood love a

free party."

He didn't look like himself tonight. I don't know what it is, but I'll get to the bottom of it later. I

continued to say, "come on, let's go inside and you can meet my aunties. They can't wait to meet you." We walked in together hand and hand, and right away, here comes my cousin with her ratchet ass and in her ratchet ass voice, she said, Hey Jai, what's up cuz? I haven't seen you in a while. A bitch all boogie now and shit."

I let go of Kas' hand and put my hands on my hips and said, "girl, ain't nothing boogie about this ass whooping I can give that ass, if you don't shut the fuck up."

Kas looked at me like, what the fuck! He's never heard me be ratchet and use so many curse words in one sentence. I continued to say, "don't let my change of address fool ya ass, ok!"

We looked at each other and bust out laughing and started hugging. After our long hug, I introduced her to Kas. "Kas, this is my little cousin Meeka, Meeka, this my boo, Kaseem."

He hugged her and kissed her on the cheek and she started blushing and shit. I quickly broke that shit up and said, "Aight bitch, that's enough with all the blushing and shit."


After walking around introducing Kas to the important family members, like my aunties and uncles and my favorite cousins, we started dancing. After our dance, I yelled in his ear, "babe, I'll be back. I'm going outside for a minute to call Mia and Topaz."

He just nodded in agreement. The music's too loud to have a normal convo. Soon as I reached outside Mia, Tone, Topaz, and Jah were all outside smoking and shit. Acting like I was mad, I tried to sound annoyed when I said, "damn! Y'all could've told a bitch y'all was out here. Me and Kas in there turning the fuck up and y'all out here partying."

Of course, Ms. Topaz, the spokesperson of the group always gotta talk and she says,

"We was coming in, it just so happened that we arrived here at the same time."

She passed me the blunt and I take a few pulls and passed it to Tone and said, "come on y'all, let's go party like it's the 90's and turn the fuck up!"

I turned around to go back inside and I heard someone calling my name. We all turned around and it was Jr.. He finally made it to his party. I started yelling down the street at him.

"Nigga, come the fuck on, how you late to your own party? This ain't no surprise nigga!"

All I saw was teeth and him grinning hard as hell. "Chill shawty, I'm coming! You know I gotta make an entrance," Hak said.

I introduced Jr. to Mia and Topaz only, because apparently Hak knows Jah and Tone. I can tell by the way they greeted each other. We all walked in together and I started screaming.

"Looks who's here!" I was screaming at the top of my lungs, but nobody but the people close enough heard me and that was enough. Once they got excited to see him, everybody knew what was going on. I was looking around for Kaseem, but I don't see him. I wonder where he went. He probably went to the bathroom, oh well it's party time. I leaned over to Mia and Topaz and said, "let's turn the fuck up!" I don't know what happened to Kaseem, I've been calling and texting him all night. I went outside for 10 minutes and when I came back he was gone. I'm looking like boo boo the fool in front of my family and my friends. I think I'm done with his ass. There is no way I can be with a motherfucker like that. I don't trust his ass, and I'm tired of looking like a fool.

# Kaseem

Damn, I know I shouldn't have left like that, but why the fuck was Jai outside hugging Hak?

As I pulled into my driveway, I was hoping that Trina was just like I left her, sleep! Just as I was taking the keys out of the ignition, my phone started to ring for the hundredth time and it's Jai.

"Hello."

Jai is yelling at the top of her lungs. "Kas, what the fuck? Why the fuck did you leave without saying shit to me? You had me looking like a fucking ass again! And I'm not tryna hear no bullshit ass excuse either."

She was cursing my ass the fuck out. After her rant, I tried to put my pity voice on and said,

"Jai, baby I'm sorry but I'm sitting at the hospital parking lot."

"For what Kas? What the fuck is going on?"

I took a deep breath and tried to sound as pathetic as possible.

"Jai, while I was dancing with your auntie, I got a text that my cousin got shot. I was in such a shock, I left out the back door because I didn't feel like explaining myself to no one just yet. I just needed to get out of there."

I know her ass don't believe shit I'm saying, but hell it's worth a try. She calmed down and in a calm voice she said, "Oh Kas, I'm sorry to hear about your cousin, but why not just tell me that on your way out the front door? You knew I was out there."

"I don't know, Jai, I just wanted to get out of there without having to talk to anyone. I needed to just go!"

"I understand Kas, but I'm your woman and it's things like that I should know. I could've went with you to the hospital, you didn't have to be alone at a time like this."

"Jai, I love you and I know I fucked up. I'm sorry, but I can't lose you, too!"

I skipped over all that shit she just said, I just needed to trust me again so I can find out what's up with her and Hak.

"Awe baby, I love you too and you're not losing me, we just have to communicate better."

Bam! Got her! That's all I needed to hear. I gotta get her to tell me the nature of her and Hak's relationship. I can't do it right now though, I gotta get in the house before Trina wakes up. She may already be up and waiting.

"Babe, I gotta run, my uncle is waving for me to come inside, I'll call you tomorrow, I love you."

# Mia

I'm in the shower washing off all the nasty shit that me and Tone did last tonight. I'm having

flashbacks about it and it has me feeling some kinda way. I put it out my mind and started washing my hair. I'm

up under the water, but I heard someone talking to me.

"Excuse me miss, I need you to step out the shower please."

I immediately covered my body and said, "who the fuck is that?"

"Ma'am this is Newark PD, please step out the shower."

I felt very violated now, why is the fucking police in my fucking house? I started yelling at they ass, "I'm not

getting outta shit, until you get the fuck out my damn bathroom!"

What the hell is going on. When I heard the door close, I peeked from behind the shower curtain and stepped

out. I put my robe on and a towel around my soapy hair. When I stepped into my living room, it was like 6 cops

standing there and Tone in handcuffs. I started yelling, "what the fuck, Tone, why you in cuffs?"

I looked at the officer holding on to Tone's cuffs and then back at Tone, and with this disappointed look he said,

"babe, call Jah." Call Jah? I'm thinking, oh shit, this must be serious if he telling me to call Jah. I'm really

scared now.

"What's going on and why y'all locking him up?"

Ain't nobody saying shit, and Tone acting like this some normal shit, because he ain't saying shit either. Before

I could ask another question the cops says, "Ma'am he has a warrant, you can call the precinct in about an hour

to find out what his bail is."

"Ok." I kissed Tone and said, "don't worry, baby I'mma get you out."

Tone didn't respond to what I said. The only thing he said was,

"Call Jah, I love you."

As they escorted him out the house into the car, I stood there and watched them drive him away. As soon as they were out of my eyesight I began to cry. I gotta call Jah.

# Topaz

Damn, last night was everything! We had a real good time at Hak's party. It was mad real. I bet Tone and Mia still sleep too, because they were just as drunk, and we filled our lungs all night. My phone started ringing and I must have talked her up, because it was Mia calling me.

"Hey Mia pia, I'm surprised you're up."

"Erica, where's Jah?"

"He at the club why? What's wrong?" She sounded like she was crying.

"The cops just left my fucking house, and they locked Tone up."

Oh shit! I jumped up and started putting some jeans on, because I'm going to her house. I said,

"Da fuck? What they lock him up for?"

"I don't know, they said they had a warrant. Tone told me to call Jah."

Shit, if he said call Jah, then that mean it's some hood shit. I knew I shouldn't have fell in love with this nigga, he better not be caught up in no bullshit.

"Aight Mia, hold on let me call Jah on the 3 way."

**Phone ringing….**

"Speak to me."

"Babe, I got Mia on the phone and she said the cops came to her house, and locked Tone up!"

"What! For fucking what?" Jah said.

Mia was crying as she said, "I don't know, they said they had a warrant."

Ayo, Mia calm down" Jah said. "What is the warrant for?"

Mia said, "I don't know, they never said."

"Aight, relax and I'mma call our lawyer and get him out, it's gonna be aight. Topaz, can you come down to the club and finish my monthly reports for the investors while I handle this?"

Right away I answer, "babe, I don't think so. I'm going to Mia's house with her."

Mia interrupted me and said, "Topaz, it's cool, I'll meet you at the club and help with the books. I don't wanna be home anyway."

"Aight, y'all make it down and I'mma handle this, and Mia relax we good baby, you hear me?"

Mia responded yes and I hung up. On my way to the club, I'm wondering what the fuck is going on? Could Jah and Tone both be lying about going legit? I hope not.

# Kaseem

Time to meet Hak, and I'm not looking forward to it. This may be the last time I breathe air. Trina and the boys are at the mall, I'm glad I got my time with them earlier today, shit you never know. I was supposed to meet him tonight, but he texted me and said he was leaving tonight and I had to meet him earlier. Let me call the goons and get them lined up. I called Cory first, he can get things in order. "Cory, I'm going to Slicks in 45 mins. I'mma need you and the goons to set up a perimeter around Nye Ave. I want niggas on the roof and in the club."

"Aight, but who the fuck we taking out? Send me a pic or something nigga." Cory said.

"You don't need a pic nigga, it's Hak!"

"Hak? Nigga, you done lost your rabbit ass mind! The fuck we doin yo?"

"Listen, I know what I'm doing. We may not have to do shit, if things go right. I'm just covering my ass in case it goes left." I said.

"Ayo, that nigga is the fucking man, if I kill his ass how the fuck we gon eat?" Cory said.

"Nigga, have I ever put you in some shit and you not be covered? Ever?"

"Naw nigga, but this shit here is deep, deeper than I wanna be."

"No worries nigga, we good. Trust me, just line the shit up!"

# Jah

Sitting in the courtroom makes me nervous as hell. When they brought Tone out, he looked defeated. I don't like that look. He's a G, and I need him to act like it. According to the prosecutor, he was being charged with, conspiracy to distribute narcotics, with intent to sell. That's some bullshit. Where the fuck they come up with this shit. We have a great lawyer and he got Tone bail for quarter million dollars. No problem. I signed over the club and got him out.

"Tone, what the fuck man? How the fuck you get caught up yo?"

"Man, I was chilling. Big better not be in there snitching yo. How else could they know what we doing? They have a lot of evidence nigga, and witnesses. They know shit only our right hands would know. Shawn got popped, so that leaves Big." Tone said.

As much as I didn't wanna think that Big would roll over on us, who else could it be? I just shook my head and said, "if that nigga snitching, on everything I'mma kill that nigga. I wanna know who popped Shawn, too." Tone looked like he was just done with the whole shit. He said with anger in his voice,

"nigga, I told you we need to just get the fuck out while we had the chance. Now I'm about to catch another case and with the shit they got, I may be doing life, my nigga. What about what we trying do? My baby gonna be heartbroken. I promised her eternity, not life behind bars."

Tone is stressed the fuck out. All I could say was, "Tone look man, we good and you gone beat these charges. Let's go to the club, smoke a few L's, and toss back a couple of shots. Mia and Topaz are there waiting on us." He didn't seem as excited as I thought when he heard Mia's name. I guess he really fucked up, but I got him, I'mma handle everything.

# Kaseem

I walked in the club and I saw my peoples in place. Cory knows he's a straight goon.

Looking around and I see Hak over there rubbing on booties and putting dollars in tits. I sat down and ordered

my drink and wait for him to come to me. Ass shaking in my face and I get

trapped into giving away a few 20's, but it's all good. When Hak approached me, we gave each other daps and

exchanged long ass eye contact, meaning we good. We went outside to handle business, because it's loud

inside. When I moved, the goons slid out, too. When I get outside, I saw my peoples positioned where they

supposed to be. Hak lit his blunt and leaned up against his car and said, "What's good with it? How's your son

doing?"

Looking around my surroundings, I caught eye contact, and everything about this nigga say snake, but I gotta

do what I gotta do.

"He good, thanks for asking. You leaving today, huh?"

"Yeah man, I was turned up last night, bruh. My cousin gave me a party last night at the center and it was

lit.""Oh word, that's what's up. Damn, you ain't even invite a nigga. I would've came out and turn't up with

you."He passed me the blunt this time. I guess we cool again since I'm here to pay my debt. He continued to

say, "nah nigga, you know I would've invited you, but my cousin Jai was doing that invite shit, her and my

momma."

Oh shit, Jai is his cousin! Now I know the nature of that hug! But damn, if this nigga knew I was tryna play his family out, he's really gonna kill my ass. Fo sho! This nigga can't find out or I'm dead for real. "It's all good." I said. I gave him back the blunt and said, "yo, let's walk to my car and do the damn thing. I gotta get back home to the wife."As we walking, I saw the goons moving. Them niggas on point too. I opened the trunk and gave him the bag. Before he could say anything, I said, "Hak, this is 40 and I'll give you the other 10 in a couple of weeks."

He tossed the fucking blunt and he started looking around, but he didn't see my goons. He walked up on me real close and said, "nigga, didn't I tell you I want all my money at one time?"

"Nah, what you said was you didn't want any guns. Look I'm trying nigga, I got other motherfuckers I owe too."

"Didn't Tone get knocked today?" He said.

"Shit, I don't know, this the first time I'm hearing that."

"Word on the street is the nigga about to do football numbers in the feds," he said.

Fuck all that, I don't give a fuck about that right now, I'm trying to save my ass. I didn't even touch that fucking Tone subject, I just looked at Hak and said, "So, what's up? We good or nah?"

Yeah, we good nigga, just see me next week and we really good."

"Aight, bet! I gotta go, but I'mma see you."

As soon as I got into my car, Cory called and confirmed that I was good. I asked Cory about Tone getting knocked off and he confirmed it to be true. All I'm thinking is, one down and one mo to go. Time to go and work Jai for this 10 G's.

# Jai

I can't believe Tone got locked up on those fed charges. I'm glad Jah got him out though. Mia and Topaz both were driving me crazy. I'm so happy I don't have to deal with shit like that when it comes to Kas. He's supposed to be coming to hang out with me today while I work on some sketches for the seamstress. Speak of the devil, here he comes walking in like he owned the place. "Hey baby, what's up?" I said.

"Hey, babe," he said, as he sat down on my lounge sofa.

"You ok? How's the family dealing with your loss?" I stopped sketching and went over to sit on his lap. He didn't respond right away, so I knew something else was up.

"What's up babe, you good?" I said.

"Jai, nah I'm not good, not only did my cousin get popped, but now my last investor has backed out of my deal, and I'm only 10 grand from starting my own company. I'm so tired and frustrated about this whole shit. I'm about to say, fuck it! I'll just keep working for the man and make his ass rich." Feeling bad for my baby, I knew he wanted this really bad, and he was so close, too. I hate to see him feeling defeated. I know I can help him, and make some money at the same time.

"Baby, what if I invested in you and your company? What would be my return?" I said.

He started kissing me and said, "baby for real, you'll invest in me?"

I kissed his forehead and said, "yes, baby, I will. It's an investment in our future."

He looked so excited! Like a kid on Christmas day, he stretched his arms, grabbed me, and whispered, "Go lock the door. I wanna show you just how much I love and appreciate you."

I hauled ass to the door and before I could turn around good, he was standing in front of me. Good thing I have plenty of clothes, because he ripped my shirt off and sucked on my tits like a starving infant. He picked me up and carried me to the sofa and pulled my skirt up. He took my panties off and began kissing my pussy lips. He was making love to my pussy. His tongue was going in and out real slow. He sucked on me until I creamed all over his face. He wasn't done, he stood up and got ass naked. His dick was hard as hell and he looked so good, I couldn't help but suck his dick. I sucked his shit so good, the nigga was screaming. I knew it was good when the nigga screamed he loved me. After he came, I swallowed all of that nut and wiped my mouth like I had a meal. The shit turned him on so much, he started pounding this pussy. He was still hard when he pulled me up and bent me over my desk and fucked the shit outta me. I came real fast and he kept going. Damn, that monster dick on point today. After he got finish banging my brains out, we laid on the floor draped in fabric, smoking a blunt. He turned to me and said,

"Jai, I love you, and thanks for believing in me."

# Topaz

Jah has some explaining to do, we haven't talked about the Tone situation since it happened the other day. I know he knows that I'm not feeling it. We have had many conversations about the street life and how I want no parts of it. Walking into the club, I see DJ Snaxx in the booth setting up for tonight. "Hey fav, what's up? You here early. You wanna hear some of your favorites tonight, or nah?"

"Hey Snaxx, of course I do. You know you my favorite DJ, I'll holla at you later. Is Jah in his office?"

"Yes ma'am he is. The boss always in his office."

I walked in to see Jah on his phone cursing. "Nigga, I don't give a fuck about none of that. You better get yo ass out there and find out what I need, like asap. And if I gotta come through the hood, you know I will and it won't be no pleasant visit, my nigga!"

Jah is in rare form; I have never seen him like this before. Well, he's about to be extra mad because I came prepared for a fight.

"Hey baby, you look stressed."

"I am babe, I'm tryna figure out who the fuck got it out for me and Tone. It's too much shit happening, and I need answers. All we tryna do is go legit."

"Are you really, Jah? From the looks of shit, y'all still in deep as hell. I'm not feeling this shit at all and I'm nervous about coming to the club now and everything."

"Really, Topaz? You gon' come in here and tell me some bullshit like this, knowing I got enough on my plate. So what you wanna do, leave me? If that's it, you could've called and said that shit on the fucking phone!"

"Fuck you, Jah! I know you got shit going on, but you don't have to take the shit out on me. I did nothing but love your ass, and all I want from you is honesty. The same shit I've been asking for since day 1 and you promised me that you were."

Jah was really mad, he stood up, and jumped in my face and said, "you want honesty? Ok, here it go. I fucking love you woman and there is nothing in this world that I wouldn't do for you. I have a past and it's hard to leave. Do I wanna leave? Yes, but can I leave? No, and I'mma do what I have to do to stay in business, legal business. That means I still gotta hustle to keep money flowing. Topaz, stop acting like you don't know shit. You from the fucking hood too, or

did you forget that shit?"


I'm so mad right now I started crying. I can't believe I fell for the bullshit! I should've known he was still in it. I think deep inside I knew, but I loved him. Only thing I could say was, "Jah, I didn't sign up for this. I'm scared that I'mma lose you." He grabbed me by my face and said, "babe, I'm not going anywhere, just trust me, we gon be alright. Everything will be alright."

He pulled me in real close, kissed my forehead, and held me until I stopped crying. As I was pulling away, I glanced at the monitors and saw the police coming in the club.

"Jah, the police are coming in!" He spun around and looked at the monitors. He quickly opened his safe and gave me all the cash to put in my purse and he had a cell phone too. He said, "Topaz, don't say shit. You don't know shit. Stay calm and call Tone." I'm scared as hell; I don't know what to do. I'mma just do what

I'm told. The manager knocked on the door and Jah grabbed me and kissed me hard as hell. Still in his arms he, said, "come in."

The manager walked in with about 3 cops, and I'm scared shitless. Jah looked at them and said, "How can I help you, officers?" They responded by saying, "Mr. Morton, you're not under arrest. You are wanted for questioning. We were sent here to escort you downtown." Jah said with anger, "y'all could've called and said that shit! I know where the fucking police station at."

I looked at Jah like, nigga calm down. He returned the look like, shut the fuck up. Jah simply kissed me and said, "babe, I'll be back just relax here until I get back. Tell Tone to come open the club up while I handle this." That was code talk for call Tone and tell him what's up. I said ok and they left. What the fuck have I gotten myself into.

# Kaseem

I paid Hak back his money and I'm good with him, thanks to his cousin, Jai. I gotta figure out a way to keep

them niggas, Jahmar and Tone locked the fuck up. I keep giving the police information, damn near handed them

niggas over on a platter, and they still managed to slip through, the fuck I gotta do? I might have to kill these

niggas. I dropped the dime on Big, and stole his fucking shit while he was locked up, thanks to Cory. That's

how I paid Hak the first 40 grand. Big came home and I had Cory tell this nigga that Shawn snitched on his ass.

In return, Big killed Shawn. I needed that to happen because Shawn was the hitter, he would shoot anything

moving. I couldn't allow him to live, cuz Tone and Jah would use him to wipe out my whole family. I don't

plan on giving them nigga's shit. Not after they robbed me and put me outta commission and totally

disrespected me in front of my homies, making me look like a punk. Fuck them! Not only will I kill ya mans,

but I will take over the entire city, nigga. The city that they run, I'mma run errthang. Nah, I'm not gonna

kill'em. I want them to stay alive in jail, and watch how I take ova they shit. They tryna go legit! Hell, fucking

no, nigga. Everything they try, I'mma fuck it up; believe that shit! Fuck them fuck boys! I got an inside man

too, Cory gone be my right hand when the takeover is done. He been putting in mad work for me. I got nothing

but respect for that little nigga. He got heart.

# Topaz

This was some straight bullshit! I can't believe I'm with a fucking hustler again. It is what it is. Jah was being questioned at the fucking police station and Tone out on bail. Jai the only one not in the middle of some bullshit. I gotta call her and see what's up with her. I haven't heard from her since Jr.'s party.

**Phone ringing…..**

"Hello, this is Jai."

"Oh bitch, you alive! Where the fuck you been?"

"Hey Erica, I been working. What's up?"

"Well damn, you know Tone got locked up?"

"Yeah, Mia told me, that's fucked up. So, what's going on with that?"

"Nothing yet, he out on bail, so we just waiting to go to court. Somebody's out to get him and Jah. How about today, while I was at the club, the police came and took Jah in for questioning. I was scared as hell."

"Oh shit! What the fuck they questioning him about?" Jai said.

"I don't know, but he said not to worry. He thinks they just fishing. A lot of shit been going on, first Big got locked up, then Shawn got killed, and let's not forget my writer, Shane, got locked up too. So it's a lot. I'm sure everything will come out once they go to court. They probably building a case against them. Whatever it is, someone is snitching and Jah is determined to find out who."

"Damn, it is a lot. I know you didn't wanna be in no shit like this and I'm sorry. So now what?" Jai said.

"I'm just waiting for Jah to come back, I'm sure he's gonna be pissed. I really don't want no parts of the bullshit. I'm in love with a fucking hustler, yo!" I took a deep sigh, and Jai said,

"Topaz, I know this ain't what you wanted, but sometimes the heart wants what the heart wants."

"Well enough about this bullshit, what's going on with you?" I said.

Jai's tone changed, in her voice she sounded so happy. She said, "well, everything is cool, just making them coins and falling deeply in love with Kaseem."

I can't believe she's even speaking to that motherfucker, after he left her ass stinking at the party, but whatever. She liked it, I loved it. I said, "awe Jai, you sound really happy and if he makes you happy, than fuck what anybody thinks, including me. I just want you to be happy."

"Erica, I am very happy. We spend a lot of time together; he treats me well. I have even helped him start his own marketing firm. I invested some money and the return on my investment is generous. I can honestly say, I love him. He's in a meeting now with a guy from LA to talk about starting up out there. So I will be doing a lot of traveling back and forth. I'm excited about it."

I'm hating a little, she got a legit man, something that I wanted. Maybe we were wrong about Kaseem, maybe he is perfect for her.

"Jai, I'm really happy for you, for real. I pray everything works out for you two. We'll have to have lunch one-day next week, soon as everything simmers down a little or maybe we can all have dinner. We can get to know Kaseem a little better, I can admit that I might have been wrong about him. I'll call you soon, I love you."

"That sounds like a plan, Erica. I love you, too," she said.

I know Jai is happy, but something is still off about him. She never explained what happened at Jr.'s party, maybe I'm just hating. Like my momma always said, whatever lies in the dark becomes truth in the light. I'm sure if he doing some bullshit, we will find out sooner or later. I'm working from home today, I just don't feel like being around people. I'm waiting on Jah to come back or call or something. I hope he's ok and that nothing comes of this so called questioning.

**Phone ringing…..**

"Baby?" I hear the sweetest voice ever. It was Jah.

"Hey daddy, you ok? I've been so worried about you. Is everything ok?"

It was a long pause before he said anything, I'm not feeling that shit, something is wrong. He took a deep breath and said, "No baby, they locking me up, and Tone came down, but it's nothing he can do unless he comes up with a half a million-dollar bail."

I laid back on the bed and started crying, but I managed to say, "For what Jah, you ain't do shit. Oh my God, how the fuck I'm supposed to get you out? I don't have that kind of money."

"Baby, I know, don't you worry about it. Tone is going to handle it. It may take a while before I'm released, but I'm coming home to you. I just need you to stand by me and believe me when I tell you, it's bullshit! We being set up. We have some serious haters out there. They trying to take us out, but its not gonna work, don't worry please. I love you and I need you to be strong."

I couldn't stop crying. All I could think was, we were finally progressing as a couple and things were perfect, so I thought. I stopped crying long enough to say, "I love you, too. Jah, what you need me to do?" I can't even believe I even asked that shit. I told myself that if he's caught up in some shit, I would leave his ass, but nope, here I am trying to help. What the fuck am I thinking? I love him, that's what I'm thinking. He said, "Topaz, I just need you to help Tone run the club, Mia will help run the restaurant. I don't wanna loose everything I worked hard for. Everything else as far as this case, I got it handled. I gotta go, listen this the only free call I'mma get, so you gonna have to add money to your phone so I can call you. I love you and I'll call you tomorrow."

"I love you, Jah and please be safe in there. Don't forget to call me tomorrow."

As soon as I hung up, I just started balling my eyes out until they were puffy and swollen. I can't believe I'm going through this shit. I gotta pull it together. I guess I'll go to the club tonight and make sure shit's running smoothly. I needed a blunt after that call. Let me call Mia and tell her to bring me a pack.

# Mia

My sista is so fucked up right now. I feel bad for her. I know exactly how she's feeling, but Tone came home in a matter of hours. So I know she stressed out not knowing when he coming home. I stayed and smoked a couple of blunts with her and I'll see her later tonight after I close the restaurant. It's like we both have extra jobs and shit. She running the club, and I'm running the restaurant. Tone out doing whatever it is he do, to get that money up for Jah's bail. While I'm in the kitchen making me a high time snack, my text notification went off and I couldn't believe what I was reading. It was that bitch ass Jayson.

*Hey beautiful, I'm in town for business and I know you probably don't wanna see me, but would you please meet me for dinner. I want to talk to you about LA and really apologize to you, Please.*

This nigga must be out his rabbit ass mind! The nerve of him, it's been months and now he wanna talk. Fuck him! That white bitch probably left his monkey ass. I hope she did. Whelp, back to my snack, I'm not even entertaining his ass, delete!

**Phone ringing……**

This better not be Jayson or I'm cursing him the fuck out. I don't recognize this number. I answer with caution, "hello?"

"You have a collect call from inmate Tone, to accept this call press 1."

Oh my fucking God, like what the fuck happened now? I pressed one and Tone was sounding defeated. "Baby, they got me for trapping, my bail has been revoked and I gotta stay until my trial. I don't have much time, I just wanted you to know what's up. I'mma call you tomorrow to fill you in."

"Baby, I need to know more. What the fuck is going on?" The fucking phone hung up. Oh my fucking God!

# Kaseem

"Thanks for meeting me tonight Jayson, I really wanna go legit and not like them other fools. They always wanna open up bars and clubs and shit. They so fucking stupid, that shit is a front for illegal activities and everybody knows that shit. Including the cops. That's why I was happy you decided to help me."

"Hey, it's not a problem, I'm always willing to help a brother out, especially if he tryna do right. I mean the way we went about it, may be fucked up, but sometimes you gotta take a loss."

I'm sitting in the cigar bar at Savoy's, where it all started and it's almost ending. Jayson and I met to discuss our next move in the 'takeover'. Once I told him that Jai told me that she suspected Mia was fucking Tone, I knew I could use that info to my advantage. I just didn't expect Mia to break up with Jayson so soon. It worked out for me anyway, because that made him angry and he wanted revenge. I knew I could count on Jai to keep telling me shit. All I had to do was fuck her good and tell her I loved her and she would continue to talk. Jayson made the phone call and got Tone knocked off again and now Mia's single, just like he wanted. I had Shawn killed because I knew that would take Jah off his game a little, and he would be overcome with grief. Besides that, Shawn was getting hip to Cory and I couldn't lose my main man. He is my inside connect. Cory's doing his job and had one of his loyal customers finger Jah as the kingpin and it wasn't hard to prove. He gave the bitch a fucking phone and recorded the transactions between them. It was sweet too, because this the bitch get high but she makes big drops for Tone and Jah for a nice package for herself. She was a mule, she would travel and pick up packages from Hak and bring it back to them. For a little extra coke, she agreed to make the tape and drop it off to the police. Now that them niggas locked up, I'm getting all the cash flow, which allows me to really go legit with my family. Once I'm up and running, I'mma cut Jai loose. I could really do it now, but I need to wait until this trial is over, and them niggas is away for life. Jayson and I discussed business for about an hour. Things were going good until I got a call. I answered, "what's up?"

"ayo Kas, this Mal, the cops just rolled up on Cory yo, they taking him to 7th precinct for questioning."

"The fuck? Question him about what?" I asked.

"I don't know man, he told me to call you."

"Aight yo, good looking."

What the fuck? Why in the hell would they wanna question Cory? I can't go down there, I'mma have to wait this one out. I can't be nowhere near this shit. I ended my meeting with

Jayson. I'mma just go home and wait for Cory to call me and let me know what's up. I'm not letting him sit. Jah and Tone locked up, so I gotta go snatch him, but I'mma send a fiend to bail him out. I need to know what's up.

# Topaz

Dj Snaxx is on the one's and two's, and the club is lit. It's business as usual. Meanwhile, Jah sitting in some jail cell. I'm so unhappy right now. I'm going to see him tomorrow, hopefully he has some good news for me. I don't know what we gonna do now that Tone is locked up. Half a mil is something I don't have and what I'm not doing, is putting up anything I own. I'm in love, but I'm not stupid. Mia got a lot on her plate too. We are both in the same situation. To my surprise, Jai is happy and happy with Kaseem. After closing down the club I went home, smoked a blunt to the head so I could go to sleep, and start over again in the morning. It's been a long day. I can't wait to see Jah, I miss him so much already.

The next day, I was sitting in this dirty ass waiting room, with a bunch of women dressed like they going to the club and hollering kids. I will not be doing this shit for too long. As I'm sitting waiting for my name to be called, guess who walked in? Mia! "Mia, I didn't know you were coming here today, why didn't you call me?" Pulling her jeans up because they made her remove her belt, she sat next to me and with a deep breath she said, "I called you last night, but you didn't answer. I wanted us to come together, I'm so glad you're here." She looked around the same way I did, when I first got here.

"I would've called you, but I knew you was beat." I said. We didn't really have a chance to talk. The CO called my name and it was my turn. I'm nervous as hell. I'm in line with a bunch of other women and we are instructed to follow the officer through one bolted door. Once we are all piled in, the door slams loud behind us. Then the door in front of us opened.

We walked through a fenced cross walk with bob wires and shit, I'm scared as hell. I don't know how these niggas do it. This shit is for fuck boys, for real. Once we got to the other building, I walked into a big room full of tables and chairs. I chose a seat and waited. The officer came out and announced the no touching rules, and then the men came out. I saw all these men walking in and none of them was Jah. I didn't know what to think, but finally he walked in. I was relieved to see him, and he looked like he was ok. He was wearing a green jumpsuit. I don't know why I thought he would be in orange. But he was smiling and he looked happy to see me, too. I wanted so much to jump in his arms, just to feel him and smell him. I wanted to kiss his lips and hold his hand, but none of that was allowed. He sat across from me at the little round table and said,

"Hey baby, I miss you so much."

"I miss you, too. Jah, are you ok?"

"Baby, I'm fine. Please don't worry, this is a cake walk."

"I can't help but worry, how am I going to get you outta here?"

"Listen, Tone is down too. I don't trust anybody anymore. Everybody is suspect to me. You're the one of very few I can trust. I need you to handle some things for me."

"What things, Jah? I'm not trying to get caught up in no bullshit." I said.

"Babe, all you gotta do, is see Hak."

Shaking my head, no before he could even finish, I said, "Hell no Jah, see him for what?"

"T, listen, all you gotta do is see Hak, pick up the package, and drop it off to Spaz."

"Who the fuck is Spaz, and why the fuck can't this Spaz dude go get it?" I said, looking around making sure nobody was listening to us.

"Because I trust you. Just drop it off to Spaz and when he's done, he'll bring you the money."

"Then what? I can come bail you out?"

"No not yet, you gonna have to do at least 10 drops, and pay the workers, too."

"No Jah, that's just too much. I don't know what I'm doing. Them niggas don't know me and I don't wanna know them. Can't you find anybody else to do the shit?"

"No baby, please do this for us, if you don't I'll be in here forever. Do you know how long a motherfucker can wait for a fucking trial?"

He sounded like he getting mad. I didn't wanna stress him out any more than he already was. I guess I can do that, it's just picking up and dropping off. It's not like I'm on the block trapping and shit. "Ok Jah, what I gotta do?" I said.

"I got in touch with Hak already, and he gonna bring you some work. He's gonna show you how to do the math, so nobody cheat you. The money you get off the first pack, you gonna pay Hak back, because he's giving me the first pack on credit. Pay the workers and buy another pack from Hak. I don't know if he'll bring it to you, or if you gonna have to go get it. I'mma see if he can bring it to you, keep you from traveling, but no promises. After you get the money up, go to a bails bond and post the bail, and I'm home. Simple as that."

"Jah, nothing is ever that simple, are you sure that's all I gotta do?" I said.

"Yes, babe, trust me."

"What about Tone, how we gone get him out? Is he gonna tell Mia the same thing, when she come back here? She out front waiting."

"Tone a different story, he gotta sit. His bail was revoked. So he'll be here for a while, waiting for a trial date and then waiting to go to trial."

"How is he, is he ok?" I asked.

"Yeah, he good, he just mad cause we being set up. He's really worried that Mia gonna leave him."

"Well tell him not to worry, she not leaving him. Hell, she in the waiting room. He can put that out his mind and relax on that one." I said.

Damn, that was a quick visit. The CO announced that the visit is over.

"Jah, I love you be safe in there."

"I love you too baby, don't worry I'm good. As long as I have you, I'm good. You be safe and watch your back. I got some haters out there. Oh, and Spaz gonna be watching your every move. Just keeping you safe. He's gonna call you at the club and come there. You guys discuss how you wanna do things. You decide when and where to meet and how you wanna run shit. You runnin shit, remember that!"

The officers instructed all the inmates to stand and exit. Once it was clear, we were instructed to follow him for our exit, but I didn't see Mia. The exit procedure was different from the entry. I guess we'll compare visits later.

# Mia

Watching Tone come through that door, made my heart skip a beat. He looked broken. I wish I could just take him home and fuck the shit outta him. He sat down with his shoulders slumped. He dosen't look like the strong, confident man I know. I looked into his eyes and said,

"Hey baby, I love you."

"I love you, too." he said.

"Are you ok?"

"Hell no! I wanna be home with you. I can't believe I'm in this bullshit again. All I wanted to do was live right, and be free from this bullshit. Every time I try to do the right thing, something always fuck it up."

Feeling his pain through his words, I felt so bad because he really means what he says.

"Baby, what you need me to do?" I said.

"I don't know yet, I'm trying get my mind right. I think I wanna sell my part of the business and just get out and start fresh, without Jah."

Without Jah, they must have had a fallen out. Curious I asked, "Without Jah? But why, that's your best friend."

"I love him, but I'm trying get out and he talking like he wanna retaliate and go hard in the hood. That shit ain't nothing but a repeat cycle. My thing is this, if we trying to get out, why do all the extra shit. All that's gonna do is, make whoever tryna set us up, come back at us and then we gonna come back at them. It's a revolving door and I want out."

"I understand and whatever you need me to do, I'll do." I said.

"Right now, I just need you to hold me down while I'm in here, and take care of the businesses. I'm sure Jah told Topaz the same thing, maybe y'all can run shit until we get out. I trust you to do what's best for us because, you're invested too."

With all the madness going on, I totally forgot I had my money invested. I looked at him and said, "don't worry about it baby, I got it and you just worry about coming home to me."

After our little half an hour visit, I left feeling heartbroken. I gotta talk to Topaz, and figure out what we gonna do. Tone wants out and that's what's gonna happen.

# Jai

Cleaning my house jamming to some music on my satellite radio, and my doorbell rings. I wonder who that could be, Kaseem has a key now so I know, it's not him. Probably my sistas. They're both going through shit. I put my dust rag down and opened the door.

"Hak? What the fuck you doing here?"

"Hey cuddy, I'm in town for a couple of weeks for business. Damn! Can a nigga come in or nah?"

I was standing there with the door open. I'm in shock because I wasn't expecting him and he didn't tell me he was coming. I let him in and turned off the music. I don't see any bags, which means he ain't coming to ask me if he could stay. He moved the throw pillows to the other side of the sofa and said, "what's up, Jai, you good?"

"Yeah, I'm good." I said, looking at his ass sideways. I felt like he wanted to tell me something. He pulled out this baggy with the goods and said, "you got a wrap?"

"No, but I got my water bong." I said.

"Cuddy, you real fancy, huh?" He said, while laughing.

"Sometimes I wanna be high and don't feel like smoking and shit. I can take a couple of hits and be good. You wanna try it?"

He wanted to try it, so I went to get the bong from my room. When I came back this nigga had his motherfucking shoes off and shit. I'm like oh ok. I handed him the bong and told him how to hit it. He hit it a few times, and choked his head off.

"Damn, now that's a good hit! Shit, I like that, I'mma have to cop me one of those," he said.

I hit it a few times and we were both high as hell. I'm wondering why he here, so I asked him,

"So tell me why the fuck you here, nigga?"

"Damn, can't a nigga come and cool out with his favorite cousin?"

"Naw, nigga, what's up?" I said, shifting my head sideways, like the crackhead meme on Facebook. Before he could answer me, my phone rang and it was Kas.

"Hello, suga plum." I said, while laughing.

"Hey babe, what you doing? You busy?" He said.

"Nothing much, just coolin with my cousin."

"Oh ok well, I just wanted to come by and scoop you up. Get something to eat and shit."

Anytime Kas wanna do something, I do it because ain't no telling when I can get my time. He been so busy with getting his business started, so naturally I agreed. I'mma get rid of Hak first.

"Ok babe, that's cool, I'll see you later." I said.

Hak looked at me with the *'who the fuck was that'* look.

"Who the fuck was that, cuz? You got a new boo?" Hak said.

Grinning from ear to ear, I picked up the bong and lit it and said, "yes cuddy, a bitch got a boo. He's name is Kaseem and he's in marketing. He's actually starting his own firm. I'm an investor as well, we doing big things."

Hak didn't even say shit about what I just said, he just kept smoking and shit and then he said, That's cool cuddy, but what you know about this nigga? You sure that you could trust this nigga with your money?"

"Yeah, I'm sure, now what's up? I gotta date."

"Oh aight, well you know what type of shit Tone and Jah caught up in,. Ya girls Mia and Topaz gonna be running shit until they get out. I'm gonna be giving them work, and to keep them as clean as possible, I'mma bring them the work. I need a place to squat for a couple of weeks. You know I'm not going to the hood."

"Nah nigga, you not bringing that shit in my house! I don't give a fuck who it's for."

"Come on now, cuz, I won't even bring it in the house. I'll leave it in the garage or basement. You won't even see it. Look if ya peoples get pulled over with that shit, we talking trafficking. I know you don't wanna see your girls down at the county."

He had a point, but I really didn't like it. I'mma let him stay, but he better not have that shit in my fucking

house! "Aight, yo but nothing in my house and no fucking either, take ya bitches to the telly." I said.

I gotta go get ready. I left his ass on the couch high and I prepared myself to go out with my baby.

# Kaseem

The fuck, man! I hope Jai didn't mention me to Hak. I know that's who she was talking about. That nigga gonna ruin everything, once he finds out Jai gave me that money. When I see her tonight I'mma find out exactly what she told him. I don't know what happen to Cory's ass. That nigga was locked up for 2 days and he was released. I didn't have to bail him out. I need to know what the fuck the cops was asking him. He better not have snitched on a nigga. I think it was real suspect that this nigga just up and disappeared after he was released. I'm on top right now, and I damn sure don't need nobody fucking up my shit. My boys got work and they pushing hard as hell, without any conflict. Jah and Tone being locked up, has paid off tremendously. No interference and no hassle. I got Jayson helping me start my business and Jai being loyal as fuck. I got about 50 grand from her so far. I think I'mma have to let her go real soon, because she's too close to Hak, it's a matter of time before he tells her some shit about me, or she talks about me and Hak finds out I used his cousin for the loot. I walk in Savoy's and was seated. I ordered my drink and told the waiter to bring a glass of wine for Jai. She called me and told me that she would meet me here. She said she needed to stop by her office first. As soon as I finished my first drink, I decided to go upstairs to the cigar bar for a smoke. I had about 20 minutes to kill before Jai arrived. While toking, I heard this voice coming from behind me.

"What's good with it, my nigga?"

Oh shit, it's Hak!

"What's good with it, my dude." I said.

He sat down and called for the lady to purchase him a cigar. I'm looking at him wondering what the fuck he's doing here. I hope Jai didn't say shit. He lit his cigar, took a pull, and said,

"ayo, I know you got that money from my cousin, so she the *bitch* you was talking about, huh?"

"Nah yo, Jai and I are just friends, she the homie." I said.

"Nigga, who the fuck you think you talking to? That's my motherfucking cousin, she's like my fucking sister! She told me that you her dude. She also said she invested in your so called business, question is should I kill you now or later?"

I'm looking around and shit, because this shit may be a fucking set up.

"Ayo Hak man, I love her and I'm leaving Trina, I just need a little time to do it. I didn't use her for her money. I'm really starting my own marketing firm. I just need to get my paper up, which is why I'm still hustling. But no way, shape, or form, am I using her." I sounded like I was pleading for my life.

"Nigga, who the fuck you think you talking to? This is what's gonna happen, number one you gone give her all her fucking money back, plus interest nigga. Then you gone stop seeing her, or I'mma kill yo ass, for real!"

He got up and left and just like that, the conversation was over. Damn a nigga gotta do it, or my boys won't have a daddy. Fuck dinner, I'm out! I gotta hurry up and make moves, and get me and my family out to LA. I'm done! I need to see Cory. Where this nigga at?

# Jah

Everything is running smooth so far. Topaz has made two drops already and now the money should be rolling in. I'm on my way to the yard, me and Tone's meeting place.

"My brother." I said, as I walked up to Tone, who is lifting weights.

"What's up, my dude? " He stood up and we started walking around the yard.

"Jah, is everything handled that we talked about?"

Checking my surroundings before I spoke, "yeah, we good Spaz took care of Cory, and Topaz stacking." I said.

"I can't believe that little nigga Cory was a snitch yo. Who would've ever thought that nigga was working for Kaseem. That nigga is behind the whole operation."

"It's cool, Tone. I'mma show that nigga who he really fucking with. I'mma kill that motherfucker, and run the whole shit again."

Tone stopped walking and looked me in my eyes and said, "yo my dude, listen, I ain't trying to be in no damn hood war! I just wanna sell my part of the business and be out! You and Topaz can run that shit if y'all want, but me and Mia are out!" This nigga crazy, but whatever. I started walking and said, "If that's what you really want, aight bruh, I'm not gonna stop you." I said.

"So yo, how the fuck you found out that Cory was a snitch?" Tone said.

"Well first of all, you remember that dude Shane who works for Topaz at that magazine? He was fucking Cory's sister, and him and Cory use to be smoking and shit and Cory started running his mouth to Shane. That's how that motherfucker did that story, but he was sure not to put me in it for a reason. Which was so Kaseem could so call handle me and I could look like the snitch."

We both laughed at the shit. Tone said, "The fuck he mean, *handle you?*"

"I don't know nigga, but I'm gonna handle his ass. Anyway, when Cory got knocked and he came through the bullpen," (county jail), "I started asking questions, and I told this nigga that I had somebody on the street bringing me back information, and that I was about to find out who set me up. The nigga got scared and started spilling his fucking guts. Not only did him and Kaseem make Big kill Shawn, but he was the one to call and drop the dime on Big, and Kaseem punk ass robbed the trap house. Check this shit out though, Kaseem really trying to go legit and he hooked up with Jayson, Mia's ex. That nigga was the one to drop the dime on you, because he found out from Kaseem, that you and Mia was fucking around, now Kaseem and Jayson supposed to be business partners."

"The fuck, yo this nigga gotta go. I could be facing some serious fucking time, because this nigga didn't know how to keep his fucking woman. This some bullshit." Tone said.

"I know, but guess what else I found out? I found out that, Kaseem got money from Jai to pay Hak back and start his business. This nigga is also married with two fucking kids. Jai has no idea he married and he's just using her and plans on leaving her ass."

Tone was mad as hell, his eyebrows are frowned up, and it looked like he was thinking hard as hell. He finally spoke and said, "yo I'm about to fuck his whole world up. I'm telling Mia this nigga married with two fucking kids and that way she'll tell Jai. Jai's ass probably gonna be so mad, that she finds his wife and tells on that ass. Then I'm gonna inform Hak that he played Jai out and that nigga crazy. He might just do what we need him to do without even asking."

As Tone is talking, I'm trying to think of a master plan. Then it hits me.

"Ayo, you tell Mia, but don't say shit to Hak. When Topaz bails me out, I'm gonna handle Kaseem's ass. That nigga gonna pay big time, him and that fucking Jayson. Kaseem won't even see it coming since his snitch is in the Passaic River, feeding the fucking fishes. No worries, bruh. I got you covered, that damn Jayson gonna be sorry as hell, trust me! When I get out, I'm gone send you a nice package."

We heard the siren going off indicating it's time to go. We dapped and parted ways. I wish we were on the same tier though. But it's cool, we'll be home soon enough and we'll be running shit again.

# Jai

I don't know what the fuck is going on with Kas, but I went to Savoy's and he wasn't there. The

waiter took me to his table, and got me seated. He went to to get Kas from the cigar bar but when he returned,

he was by himself. He said, "I'm sorry Ms., but, it looks like Mr. Melvin has left."

"Left? What the fuck?" I sat there and gave the room a quick once over, and I didn't see his ass. I

looked at the waiter, and he lowered his eyes, like he felt sorry for my ass. I said, "ok well, let me have the

steamed clams and mussels with Penne pasta, and please bring me a glass of white wine, thanks." Fuck him! He

better have a damn good reason for standing me up. He had the nerve to order me red wine! Nigga know I drink

white.

# Mia

I'm on my way to meet with Topaz, we have to talk about this hustling shit. She got motherfuckers coming into Gems looking to cop shit. They come in and take up seating and only order fucking appetizers. Most of the time it's the fucking chicken wings. The cheapest shit on the menu. I'mma need her to keep that shit at the fucking club. As I walked in I saw DJ Snaxx setting up for tonight, and the barmaids looked busy. The business was doing well, and she has made more than enough to bail Jah out. I wanna know why she hasn't done it yet. I need him to come home so we can sell him our part of both businesses. He need to be here to run them. This money getting to her fucking head. I knocked and walked in the office at the same time. She was sitting down with Spaz. He turned around and looked at me and said, "hello, Ms. Mia."

"Hey, Spaz." I said.

He looked back at Topaz, stood up and said, "Ok T, I'mma holla at you later."

I saw him put a bunch of money in his pockets and he left. That's the shit I'm talking about. She sitting up here like the ultimate trap queen. I put my purse down in the chair and sat down.

"What's up, Mia pia?" She said.

"What's up, poops?" I said, trying not to sound angry.

She sat back and lit her blunt and passed it to me and said, "How's Gems? I know business is popping."

After I passed her the blunt I said, "Yeah, business is alright that's what I'm here to talk to you about. Topaz, you gotta stop sending ya peoples over to Gems to cop. They fucking with my business. The regular customers not coming in anymore."

She was lookin real unbothered and said, "Mia, first off those aren't my people and they not coping. They picking up packages, don't act like I'm nickel and diming. I'm making everyone good money. What's the problem? Whatever you slacking in customers, you make up in profit from those packages, if not more than what you made off the ones you claim you lost."

That shit pissed me off. She acted like I'm lying about losing customers. I could strangle her ass. I stood up and looked in her face and said, "what the fuck wrong with you, Topaz? This is not the woman I remember. You're letting this fast money get in your head. Remember, this ain't even your money!"

I grabbed my purse, I didn't even wanna talk anymore. I didn't even get my answer that I came for, but I will. Heading to the door, I stopped and said, "What about, Jah? We been made enough to get him out. Why he still in jail? At least your man get to come home, Topaz!"

She must have saw the anger and hurt in my eyes. She came from behind that desk and said,

"First, let's calm down for a minute, sit down and let's talk. First off, I just gave Spaz the money to deposit so I can go and bail Jah out in the morning. Number two, I love you, let's not let this thing come between us. We got caught up and I'm doing the best I can do. Yes, I like the money. Yes, I like the power, but I'm grounded believe that. As soon as Jah comes home, I'm out! You'll be out, too. You and Tone can sell y'all part and be out."

She grabbed my face and said, "Mia, don't worry, Tone's coming home soon."

We hugged and I left. I didn't feel like I believed her for some reason. I sat in my car for about 20 minutes, trying to get myself together. I missed Tone so much. Seeing Jah home after all these weeks will seem odd without Tone. My phone started ringing, and ooh shit, it's Tone. I quickly answered that shit. That little prompt shit seemed like it was on slow motion or some shit.

After making my selection, I quickly say, "hello, baby! I was just thinking about you!"

"Hey baby, I miss you!" Tone said.

"I miss you too babe, you ok?"

"Yes, I'm fine, I have a few things to tell you."

I don't know if I'm ready to hear this, he don't sound too good. Please don't be bad news. I said a quick prayer and said, "What's that, bae?"

"First, I go to court next week, I'm happy about that." Tone said.

"That's great news baby, hopefully it will be a speedy trial, I need you home."

"I know babe, I wanna be home. Hopefully it won't be long. The other thing I needed to tell you is, that nigga Kaseem is the one who setting me and Jah up."

"What? How you know?" I said.

"I can't go into details; just know we know. Jah will handle it, here's the crazy part, that nigga married with two kids, and used Jai for her money to pay back debts he owed, and he even got money from her and he said he was using it for his business, but he used it to buy packages."

I'm sitting there with my mouth wide open, I'm in such shock. All I could say was, "get the fuck outta here! I knew that nigga was fugazy! Oh my God, Jai gonna be so hurt."

Tone was silent as hell, like he got something else to say. I started pulling my key out the ignition, I'm going back inside to tell Topaz what I was just told. She gone be mad as hell. As I get out Tone says, "Mia, there is something else too, Kaseem's business partner is Jayson! Jayson is the one who called the cops on me, and got me caught dropping packages. He's the reason I'm in here!" I almost passed out! I dropped my arms to my side, like I was knocked out with a one/two punch. "What?" I said. I needed to make sure I heard him right. He repeated it. I'm fucking mad now! "No, the fuck he didn't? I'mma kill that son of a bitch!"

"Mia, don't do or say anything, we got this. Just relax and carry on like usual."

This nigga got me all the way fucked up! I'm gonna kill his ass. That nigga lucky he in LA and I can't leave right now because of the business, but trust me, I'm gonna make a trip to LA.

My time is up with Tone on the phone.

"I love you Tone, be safe in there."

"I love you too Mia, and remember relax, and carry on. Don't le….."

The phone hung up before he could finish. I hauled ass back in the club to tell Topaz.

# Jai

I don't know what the fuck happened to Kaseem, he didn't answer the phone, and the other day I got a huge

deposit into our joint account and he took himself off the account. I think he just up and left me. I needed

answers. I been walking around here moping. I'm so heartbroken. How could he do this to me? What the fuck

did I do? I went to his house, but it was cleaned out, and there was a man there, who said that he was the

landlord and his renter just moved out a couple of weeks ago. That motherfucker lied! I'm guessing he lied

about a lot of shit. I just started crying thinking about the whole thing. How could I not see that he was full of

shit. I feel like such a fucking fool, at least he was decent enough to give me my money back, with interest. This

is so fucked up, I'm ashamed to even tell Mia and Topaz, they gon' be like 'I told you so bitch.' Well let me

pick myself up and get it together, I'mma take a shower and wash my hair. Then I'mma just smoke and sleep.

Before I could even take my clothes off, my doorbell rang. My heart skipped a beat, I hope it's Kaseem, and

even though I'm pissed I stillwanna see him. I ran downstairs and without looking through the peephole, I just

swung the door open.

"Hey, Jai," says Topaz.

To my surprise, it was Mia and Topaz. They never just show up. Right away I'm thinking, something is wrong.

"Hey Erica, hey Mia. What's wrong?"

"Well damn, can we come in?" Mia said.

"My bad, of course I'm just surprised to see y'all. Y'all never come over here without calling first."

They walked in with bags, I'm guessing it's some goodies. Mia walked in looking around like she was looking for something or somebody. I closed the door behind them and said, "what, or who you looking for? If you looking for Kas, that nigga ain't here! The last time I was

supposed to see his ass, I was eating alone at Savoy's."

They both standing there looking like they heard this before. I looked at the both of them and said, "Yo, what's up? Y'all don't look surprised or mad, shit."I sat down waiting for them to put down the bags and say something. I guess Topaz the spokesperson today. She said, "Jai, we just got finish talking to Jah and Tone, and they said that Kaseem is the one who is setting them

up. He had Shawn killed, and Big locked up."

Mia started moving in fast motion, taking food out the bags and saying, "Kaseem is supposed to be opening a marketing firm."

I looked and said, "I know, I invested into the company."

"No, the fuck you didn't give that nigga no money bitch?" Mia said, slamming the containers on the table.

"Yes, I did, but he gave me the money back, plus interest." I said.

"Jai, why didn't you talk to us first?" Mia said, as she sat down, like I just gave her bad news, or like she about to give me some.

"I didn't know I had to tell you what I do with my money, before I did it. I don't recall y'all asking me or telling me y'all was going into business with Jah and Tone." I said, rolling my eyes. I picked up a container to look at what they brought over. Mia snatched the bag and said,

"well Jai, the difference is we know them niggas. How long did you know Kaseem? And so you just gonna skip over the fact that he set them the fuck up?"

"No Mia, I'm not! First of all, the motherfucker is a snake. He left me and didn't even tell me he was leaving! We were good. I don't know what happened. He gave me all money back from my

investment plus interest. The thing that has me fucked up, is how that fucking house he was living in was a fucking rental. I don't know what the fuck happened, the motherfucker been lying from day fucking one."

I started crying, and I was trying not to, but I couldn't stop the tears. Topaz wrapped her arms around me and whispered,

"Fuck him, Jai! He don't deserve you."

"Fuck him girl, you know that he had the nerve to be partnering up with Jayson?" Mia said, while she was rolling a blunt.

I picked my head up off Topaz's shoulder and said, "what? The fuck you mean? Oh, hold the fuck up, he told me that his new partner was from LA, but never did I ever think it was Jayson." I said.

Mia lit the blunt and continued to say, "Well it was or is, but this the motherfucking killer right here, you ready? Jayson called the cops on Tone and told them about him hustling, gave name, dates, places, and times. Just straight snitched on him. Kaseem's ass gave him all the fucking information to tell. So yeah, fuck him!"

Mia was pissed! She started crying too. I know she misses Tone. I wish I never had met him and brought him into our lives, I feel fucked up. Topaz got up and comforted Mia, now. She's always been the strong one. After Mia calms down, she dries her eyes and finish smoking the blunt. We kinda just sat quietly for a minute, eating black beans and rice with roast pork. Mia passed the blunt and we all took about 2 pulls and Topaz put her plate down and said, "Jai, Kaseem is married with 2 kids!"

I spit my food out! "What? What fuck you talking about married?" I said.

"Just what I said, married with kids! 2 kids to be exact!" Topaz said, while smoking! She took one pull and passed it to me, I didn't even feel like smoking, I sat there holding the blunt shaking my head.

# Topaz

I'm on my home from Jai's house, and all I can think about is the pain that she's in. I feel so bad for her. When we left, she was curled up in the fetal position in her bed, crying herself to sleep. She said she wanted to be alone. As I pulled into my driveway, I get a text from Spaz, *I got him and we going to the club first, then I'm bringing him to you.* I was happy as hell that Jah was home. This gave me a chance to get myself together. I'm gonna fuck the shit outta him. I missed my baby so much, but why the fuck he going to the club first? Everything is handled, I took care of business like a boss, he should be hauling ass to me so he can blow my back out. I ain't gone trip though, but he better hurry up!

# Jah

Damn, fresh fucking air! I was happy as hell to be home, I got a few things I gotta handle. First thing is sending my lawyer to get Shane out of jail. That nigga a true G. He was the one to tell me to ask Cory about Kaseem. He knew that nigga was a snitch. I should've been read that damn article he wrote for my baby's magazine. I could've avoided all this shit a long time ago. After that I gotta make sure the homies are all eating, not saying I don't trust my baby, but she new to the game and I put her in an awkward position, I'm just making sure the money right. Then last but not least, I'm gonna make that nigga Kaseem suffer, him and that bitch ass, Jayson. They got my boy hemmed up and he facing 15years. Truth be told, they gonna convict him. We not telling Mia because, we don't want her stressed the fuck out. She gonna have plenty of time to do that after the trial. The goal is to get him as little time as possible without snitching. After arriving at the club, I went to my office and checked the books and the safe. What I found was unbelievable, I sat at my desk and called Topaz real quick.

"Hey baby, I'm waiting for you." She said, with excitement in her voice.

"Hey baby, I fucking miss ya ass like crazy. I'm coming, I just stopped by the club for a second and I needed to pick up my car."

"Well hurry up, baby, I miss you. Don't make me come down to that club and suck ya dick!" She said. My dick got hard as hell thinking about that warm mouth wrapped around my dick.

"I'm coming, baby, I called to say thank you and I'm gonna show you my appreciation. You better be ass naked when I walk in the fucking door."

She giggled like a little school girl and hung up. I didn't even get a chance to tell her that I saw she was a fucking boss, she got me out, paid the homies, and still managed to put up an extra 75 g's. The woman is the fucking truth. I'mma show her just how much I love her. Now to get my head back in the game, let me put some shit in the works for them snitch ass niggas, Kas and Jayson.

# Kaseem

Damn, I don't know what to do with myself. I had to cut Jai off or be dead. I feel bad for her, I know she wanted to be with me, and I was gonna keep her as long as I could keep up the lies. It would've been easy too, because we were moving to LA. Jai would never leave Jersey, I could've had a place to rest whenever I came into town and somebody to give me that bomb ass head. Damn! I'mma miss her. Trina was finally happy, she thought that us moving to LA was gonna stop my hustle, but in actuality I'm still gonna be in business. I'mma put Cory in position to run shit, be my right hand man, if I could find this nigga. I still haven't seen or heard from him. Jayson got a nice set up for me and my family. We gone be good. As I'm sitting looking through my phone, here comes Trina.

"So, you really just gone sit there and not help me pack, huh?" She said.

Laughing out loud, I pulled her close to me and her pussy was right in my face, smelling all good and shit. I tried to pull at her shorts with my teeth, letting her know I wanted to be fed. She stepped back and said, "No Kas, we got too much to do! I need to you run to the store and grab some more tape and bubble wrap. Please go to Home Depot and come right back! No side dipping please." I slapped her on her ass and stood up. I was adjusting my sweats because my dick was hard as hell.

I licked my lips and said, "look at what you did. You really gonna send me out with a hard dick?"

"Baby, you go to the store and I promise I'mma suck that monster dick." She said.

"What time ya momma bringing the boys back?" I said.

"They not coming back until tomorrow, so we got all night. Can you please bring back something to eat, too? I want Chinese food."

Grabbing my keys and phone, I was headed to the door, when I turned and looked at her and that smile that I haven't seen in a long time. I said, "you gonna put duck sauce on my dick and suck it off?"

She kissed me and said, "whatever you want, daddy."

I left to get my queen's request. While I'm at Home Depot I get a phone call from Jayson.

"Ayo Kas, I thought you said we didn't have to worry about Tone and Jah?"

I stopped dead in my tracks, "what? We don't." I said.

"Them niggas is out of jail!" He said, nervous as hell.

"No, they not relax, and even if they were, we still good. They don't know about us."

"Listen, just check it out, I don't wanna walk into an ambush." Jayson said.

I reassured him that we good, but just to be on the safe side I'mma call JuJu, that's Cory's brother and his right hand. The last time I talked to him, he hadn't seen or heard from Cory. He said when he was released, he went on the block, but he didn't come home. Jah and Tone was locked up, so I know they ain't do nothing to him, or did they?  Let me call JuJu right quick.

"Ayo JuJu, what's good with it? You heard from Cory?"

"Nah man, and I'm shook right now. Some niggas in the hood said they saw Cory leave with Spaz, but later on, Spaz came through and when I asked him if he was with Cory, he said yeah but he dropped him in GKV."

(Georgia King Village)

"The fuck he doing in GKV?" I said.

"I don't know man, he probably got some bitch that live there," he said.

"Aight, another thing, is Jah and Tone on the street?"

"Jah is home, I seen that nigga come through with Spaz, but Tone still locked down. I heard they about to give that nigga football numbers." He said.

Damn, that nigga gonna be on some rah rah shit, I know that nigga. I gotta get the fuck outta Jersey asap. After I got everything, I went home and stayed home. I gotta think of my next move.

# Mia

I don't know what the fuck Topaz and Jah doing, but to tell me they can't buy us out, is bullshit. They got more than enough money. Keeping us in this shit won't look good for Tone's case if we involved with Jah, who clearly is not letting go of the hood. He managed to get Topaz wrapped up in the shit too. I can't believe her ass. All that fucking talk about not being with a hood nigga, and she in it as the fucking trap queen. Tone wants out asap and they playing. I checked on Jai and she's doing better. She just needed her space and I can respect that. Tone's trial starts in a couple of days and I'm tryna make this transaction quick. Let me talk to Topaz again, but this time I'm I'mma keep it 100. "Hello, this is Topaz."

"Oh, bitch you know it's me." I said.

"Hey Mia pia, I didn't look at the phone, I just answered it. I'm trying to edit this article for next month. What's up?"

I'm glad she working her regular job again. That other shit was making her head big as hell.

"Erica, I'mma need you and Jah to find a buyer for our share. It's not cool to keep us a part of shit we don't wanna be a part of."

"You're right Mia, but it's hard. Nobody wants to partner up with Jah for obvious reasons. So just hang in there with us until we manage to do it alone. It won't take long, Jah's making big moves and shit running smoothly." Topaz said.

Yeah, smoothly for her ass.

Angry I said, "Topaz, that's some bullshit! You ain't pressed cause it ain't Jah. Had it been him you would move through hell and high water. So, it's fuck Tone?"

"Mia, no it's not fuck Tone, but what you want me to do? This their shit, I have no say so."

"Oh, now the fucking trap queen has no fucking say so?"

I'm mad as hell now and I don't give a fuck how she feels. I continued to say,"Y'all riding around here like the fucking king and queens of Newark and shit! Meanwhile, I ain't heard

shit about getting Tone out. As far as the money goes, y'all got it! You riding around in a new Benz courtesy of ya man, but you can't buy us out? Bullshit, and you know it!"

"Mia, first of all, I fucking earned that fucking car, and you deserve something, too."

"All I want is to be let out of the business, can you do that shit? Fuck a car, I got one of those already!"

She didn't say shit for like half a minute and then said, "Mia, I hear you, I'mma talk to Jah and see where we at, don't forget we paying for Tone's lawyer and all the shit needed to get him released. Nobody forgetting about him, especially Jah. Every move he makes is for Tone. He wanna get out the street game too, but can't. It's not just y'all." S

he fucking lying, Tone told me that Jah is in it deep and plans on staying in it. He loves that shit. I'm tired and don't even want to talk about it anymore. I'mma just wait for Tone to come home and then we'll figure it out. I just ended the convo by telling Ms. Topaz I had a client and had to go. I'm super pissed.

# Kaseem

I sent Trina and the boys to LA and I'mma go out there tomorrow. I gotta get rid of Spaz first. This nigga been doing all the dirty work for Jah. The last thing I want him to do, is get at me and mine. If I get rid of his ass, I'm good. Jah never puts in work with his punk ass, so I'mma get rid of his flunky and Big too. This nigga Big will come look for a motherfucker, so he gotta go, too. I'm not staying in the old house, I want mofos to think I left for good. I'm staying at the 8 ball, the last place a nigga gonna look for me. Jayson is in town on business, and I'mma need him to be my wingman on this hit. Especially when it comes to Big, this nigga always got niggas around his ass. I need to catch him slipping or by himself. I have Jayson's ass following him, marking his every move. This nigga so predictable, Jayson did good with finding out how this nigga move. Tonight is the night I hit that Big's ass, I hope Jayson's ready. He didn't answer his phone in the last few hours, he better not have changed his mind. He's come this far he might as well see it to the end. He supposed to meet me here in an hour, I'mma just wait to see what happens.

# Jah

I'm meeting with Spaz tonight, I heard that motherfucker Kaseem was at the fucking 8 ball. That nigga ain't low. I got niggas all over the fucking city. Even niggas he fuck with, on my team, because nobody likes a snitch, and they know they gone make real money fucking with me. Fuck that nigga. I lit my blunt and watched Spaz on my camera walk in with Jayson's bitch ass. This cornball ass nigga got involved cause his fucking feelings hurt. Fuck him! Before I kill his ass I need him to tell me Kaseem's plans.

"Nigga, the fuck you doing with Kaseem ass?" I asked.

This nigga scared shitless, he barely can talk without stuttering.

"Jah, man I ain't know it was gonna get this deep. I thought it would be some simple shit. I didn't know that Tone would be looking at hard time. Kas made it seem like he just wanted to send a message and at the same time, I could get some payback on him cheating with Mia."

I got up and smacked the shit outta him and said, "nigga, you lying, why the fuck you following Big? You and I both know damn well Kaseem slow walking his ass!"

The nigga look like he about to throw up. He sat there shaking his head, and then he started spilling his guts.

"Look man, all I wanted to do was get Tone in a little trouble, and Mia could see he's not for her and she could come back to me. Kas is gonna kill Big and Spaz, leaving you out in the open to get killed and take ova ya business. He leaving in the morning and going to LA. He was gonna have JuJu take you out, Jah. I didn't want no parts, but once I gave him a loan it was like, I had to do that extra shit to get it back. Plus, he said that he would turn me into you, if I didn't help him. Look at what it got me, caught up anyway. I'm sorry yo, and he had Big kill Shawn. I didn't find that out until after the fact. I swear to God, I had nothing to do with that."

I looked at Spaz and nodded. He knew that meant I'm done with his ass. I looked at Jayson and asked, "do you know where Kas staying?" I just wanted to see if he would tell me.

"Yeah, I do, he staying at the 8 ball, why?" He said.

I slapped his ass again, "nigga, don't you ever question me. Spaz, get this nigga out my face and take his ass to Kaseem's house and leave his ass there!"

He looked scared as hell, darting his eyes back and forth between me and Spaz and said, "but Kas don't live there anymore, it's empty."

"I know nigga, get the fuck out! Spaz, after you drop his ass come back here." I said.

They were headed out the door, but then I realized I need Jayson's phone. "Hold up, gimme your phone nigga, I need it for something."

He didn't question my ass again, he just gave me the phone and they left. Now I'mma set this nigga up, talking about I don't put in no work, I'mma show ya ass, nigga.

# Kaseem

Jayson texted me and said to meet him at the shack on Elizabeth Ave. He said Big's ass is at the shack by himself and he done set up shop in the lot across the street. I got a rental with out of state plates, so nobody gonna know who hit Big. It's been a long time coming that these niggas get what they deserve. Fuck them! I was at the light about to turn into the lot and Trina was calling. I gotta answer that or she'll be calling all night. That nigga Big ain't going nowhere in the next 10 minutes. So, I answered,

"Hey baby, y'all ok?"

"Yes, we're fine. I'm just checking to make sure everything's good on your end, and that you gon' make your flight in the morning," she said.

"Yes, everything's good, I dropped off that money to ya momma and found a realtor to sell the house. We good baby, I'll see you tomorrow and we can finally start fresh and new. Kiss the boys for me and tell them I love them."

"Ok babe, I will tell them, I love you, and see you tomorrow," she said.

"I love you more!"

I swear every time I'm about to do some bullshit, Trina always calling or texting me. Anywho, let me get on with the business. I'm sitting in the lot; I get another text from Jayson. ***Big sitting in the white caddy at the***

**abandoned gas station.** That's my cue. I pulled out the lot with my lights out and pulled up right next to the nigga. When I looked into the car, it was empty. What the fuck? I looked in my rearview mirror and there was a black car behind me. It looked like Jayson's car, but why the fuck he over here? Maybe something went wrong. I got out to walk over to him. Once I got there, the window rolled down and there was an Ak47 pointed at my chest. It was Jah! Oh shit! I've been set up!

POW POW POW!

# Mia

It's Tone's court date and I'm nervous as hell, I hope my baby don't get a lot of time and, hopefully he gets time served. The lawyers say he should only get 5 years max. I can deal with that, I'm waiting in the waiting room with Jai and Topaz. Jah isn't here yet, Topaz said he was on his way. I'm glad I have my sisters with me for support. Topaz and I squashed the little beef we had together. We not letting nothing get in between our sisterhood, especially money. Jai is feeling a lot better, she's finally back to her old self and has sworn off men for a while. That fucking Kaseem left a bad taste in her mouth, I really don't blame her. Finally, Jah walked in looking like shit. I heard Topaz say, "Baby, you ok? You look like hell."

He looked around adjusting his tie, and said, "I'm fine, baby, I overslept but I made it."

We all walked in the courtroom together like a united front. When I saw Tone's mother in the courtroom, shit just got real to me. We sat and Topaz had one hand and Jai had another. The trial was long. We broke for lunch and came back. After all the testimony and witnesses, the judge was ready to make a decision. I was so nervous. The judge found him guilty, which was no surprise. When the judge gave the sentence, I almost passed out. It was like I had an outer body experience. I think I heard him say, 15 years with no parole. Topaz squeezed my hand so tight, like she was keeping me from passing out. Tone looked back at me and mouthed, *I love you.* I just ran out the courtroom and was balling. Jai came out and wrapped her arms around me and said, "I'm so sorry sis, everything's gonna be alright, trust me."

 I heard her, but didn't really hear her. All I could say was, "15 years, Jai, they gave him fucking 15 years. He didn't kill nobody, 15 fucking years."

All I could do was cry. Jah and Topaz were still in the courtroom talking to the lawyers about an appeal. I don't know exactly what any of that shit means, I just want him home. This is fucked up.

# Final Girl talk

## Topaz

I'm meeting with Jai and Mia today for lunch. It's been awhile since we had time to really talk about things. Tone's trial was too much for us to handle. We all needed a break from the madness. I was the first one to arrive at Savoy's. I ordered everyone a drink so we didn't have to wait to get right. I really missed my sisters. I can't wait to catch up. Mia walked in, looking like a million bucks. I guess so, since she finally sold her and Tone's share of the businesses. She's taking care of her man though, Tone don't want for nothing. He's living like a fucking king in the feds. Jai came in right behind her. Jai has opened another location in Woodbridge and she's focused on that. I'm proud of my sisters for picking up the broken pieces of their lives and putting them back together. As for me, I'm doing good. Jah beat his case and we are engaged. He's still hustling, but hey it is what it is, I love his ass. Once we're seated, as usual Mia, the spokesperson has got to speak first.

"So, Topaz what's good with it, homie?"

"Shut the fuck up Mia, don't talk to me like I'm one of them niggas out in the street."

Jai cleared her throat and said, "shiid, I remember when ya ass was the homie, my nigga. The big homie."

I sipped my wine and said, "Jai, I'm not for your bullshit today, so y'all heard about Jayson and Kaseem?"

Right away Jai sat up in her chair. She still hasn't heard from Kas and I know why and I'm about to tell her some bad news, Mia gonna get it too. That's why I ordered the drinks so they could be loose, and I'm sure they gone need it. Mia sipped her wine and said, "Hell no, but what about they asses? They probably in LA somewhere coolin. Kas with his wife and

kids and Jayson with his white bitch. They probably getting a kick outta fucking up our lives, just for their enjoyment."

Jai was not saying shit; she was still hurt behind Kas' shit. No one wants to hear what I have to say, so I'mma just get to it.

"Well, Kaseem and Jayson are both dead!" I said with certainty.

Jai damn near choked on her drink and Mia sat there with her mouth wide the fuck open. They not saying shit, so I continued, "remember that shooting at the gas station, well that was Kaseem. They said it was a robbery, I don't know how true that is, everybody know Kas was a snake and anybody could've done that shit. The crazy part is, they found Jayson's ass in Kaseem's house with his fucking tongue cut out his mouth. That shit crazy as hell." I said.

Mia started crying and said, "I know me and Jayson had a bad break up, but I never wanted him to die. I did love him despite the bullshit he put me through. I'm gonna miss him."

She got up and went to the ladies' room. I'm looking at Jai and all I see is sadness in her eyes.

"Jai, are you ok? I mean I know you're not ok, but I'm so sorry. Even though he was a piece of shit, you still loved him."

Mia came back and sat down, and her face is dry. She took a big gulp of her drink and ordered another one. She said, "Topaz, how you know?"

Before I could answer, Jai started raising her voice and said, "Mia, you know damn well how the fuck she know, Jah probably the one who did the shit. He killed them or had them killed. That's some bullshit. Topaz, you in love with a fucking murderer."

"Hold up Jai, I know you mad and hurt but don't be saying shit that ain't true. We don't know who did it. Spaz came in the office at the club and told us both. True, Jah ain't shed no tears, but he didn't do the shit. How about you ask fucking Jr."

She wiped her eyes and said, "why the fuck would I ask his ass? He don't even know them."

"Yes, the fuck he do, Jah told me that he found out Kas was using you for money and made him give you back ya money with interest and he told Kas to leave you alone."

"No, he didn't Topaz, you just tryna take the heat off Jah's ass."

Mia quietly said, "Jai, you can't be mad at Topaz, even if Jah did do it, Topaz didn't, and that's what happens when you do shit like Kas and Jayson was doing. They knew the fucking street code. Don't blame her. I know you mad, but Kas already fucked up your life, don't let him continue to fuck up your life by destroying what we have. His lies have gone beyond the streets."

Jai just started crying, I knew she would take this hard. I got up and wrapped my arms around her and she just let loose. It's like she needed to release. They finally got themselves together long enough to order. We ate our food and bullshitted all night. We even stepped outside and smoked a blunt. Came back in and enjoyed the live music they had showcasing tonight. It felt like old times again, I missed them so much. After our night out, I couldn't wait to go home to Jah. I was feeling nice and ready to fuck! He ate the hell outta my pussy before I left, and I'm ready to finish what he started. We kissed and hugged and parted ways. As I drove passed them, I yelled out the window, "I love you, bitches!"

Soon as I get home, I'm ready for Jah and his monster dick. I stumbled into the bedroom and sat down. Jah walked in and said, "babe, let me help you with that."

I'm sitting on the bed and I'm trying to unstrap my shoes and here comes Jah, looking sexy as hell. He sees me having a hard time with my shoes. He got on one knee and took my shoes off. Feeling relieved to be sitting up, I said, "thank you, baby."

As he stood, I unfastened his belt and unbuttoned his pants. I pulled them down and he stepped

out of them. He looked at me in a drunken daze and said, "Tee, you forgot something."

"Don't worry baby, I got you." I said.

He looked at me like he wanted to fuck the shit out of me; but not yet. I needed something to drink. I had cotton

mouth, so I told him, "Jah, bring me a glass of water please."

As he turned into the bathroom, I took my dress off and was sitting on the edge of the bed. He handed me my

water and I sipped it real slow and gave the glass back to him. When he returned, I ordered him to stand in front

of me. I took his draws off, grabbed his dick, and kissed the tip.

"Oh shit!" He moaned.

I didn't even do nothing yet, but I know my mouth is warm. I kissed it again and this time, I put his shaft in my

mouth. Licking and sucking that dick, like I was never gonna do it again. I grabbed his balls and played with

them, while I sucked that dick.

"Damn baby, you trying kill a nigga." He said.

"No baby, just wanna make you feel good."

I was returning the favor he showed me earlier. I pushed him back and stood up. I turned him around and

pushed him on the bed. I continued to suck his dick and in his drunk raspy voice he said, "sit on it baby! I want

you to fuck me!" That was like music to my ears. I love when he talks like that to me. I straddled that dick and

rode that shit like a professional horse rider. We were cummimg together, he was screaming and I was

screaming.

The shit was good as hell, but then all of a sudden I stopped and said, "Jah, you heard that?"

He was holding onto my wrist and said, "Yeah, but who the fuck is that this time of night?"

We got up and threw some clothes on. We went downstairs and the closer we got, the louder the

knocking became. Jah put on his hood voice and said, "who the fuck is it?"

He looked at me and I was a little scared. Then they answered.

"Newark Police!"

Oh shit! What the fuck??? Jah answered the door, and standing there, was five cops in the doorway. Before either of us could say anything, one of the cops asked, "Jahmar Morton?"

"Yes, how can I help you, officer?" Jah said.

They pulled out a warrant and said, "Turn around, sir."

"The fuck? A warrant? For fucking what?" Jah said.

I saw the other officers getting nervous as they placed their hands on their guns. As soon as Jah started asking questions, things started to get tense. Now, I'm getting nervous.

The cop answered Jah and said, "we have a warrant for your arrest, the charges are, drug trafficking, and possession of narcotics, with the intent to distribute, and 2 counts of murder in the first degree. Again, Mr. Morton turn around and place your hands behind your back. This can get real ugly, real fast if you don't cooperate."

Jahmar turned around and looked me in my eyes and said, "call Spaz now!"

All I'm thinking is wtf! I know better to not question him now. I just looked at him and said,

"ok baby, call me and I'll come snatch you."

"Just call Spaz! I love you."

The officer handed me his card and said, "Ma'am, you can call the station in about 45 mins to an hour, to find out what his bail is, or if there's a bail."

This is some straight bullshit!

# Epilogue

## Topaz

After they locked Jah up, I didn't know what to do. Jah was charged with a double homicide and was sentenced to 2 life terms, in other words that nigga ain't neva coming home. When Jah came home the first time, we made up the paperwork where I became his silent partner. With me buying in, he was able to buy out Mia and Tone. I am now the owner of 2 businesses, The Strip and Gems. I told Jah that I would never sell them and to keep them up and running. We are not together anymore, but I make sure he's well taken care of and he doesn't want or need anything. That's the least I could do, since he's my baby daddy! That right, about 3 weeks after Jah got sentenced, I found out I was pregnant. I always said I wanted a family, but I wanted it to be different. I sure as hell didn't plan on having a drug dealer boyfriend, or be a baby momma! That goes to show you that, no matter what you have planned, God makes all the plans. Mia is still doing her thing. Since leaving Gems, she's opened her own restaurant in Newark. Now she has a catering business and restaurant here, and the 420 lounge in LA is doing great, with plans of doing a second location. She has said, that if she opens another one out there, then she will relocate and stay out there. I want my sister to grow her business and all that good shit, but I don't want her to have to move to LA to do it! I know, it's selfish of me but so what, I'm being petty. Seriously, I think she should go and maybe she'll find her a good man. Mia's not looking for no man anyway, she's waiting for Tone. He may be released early and trust me, she's waiting on that nigga. They in love and it's cute and I'm just hating.My girl Jai, she's been doing good and still coping with the loss of Kaseem. There was a time when she wasn't speaking to me or Mia. She was really angry when she found out that Jah killed Kas. I can't blame her, I would be mad too, but Mia and I had nothing to do with that and I told her so, but that wasn't enough, so I fell back and let her breathe. She finally came around to her senses and starting speaking to us again. She even apologized for her treatment towards us. I love my sisters and at the end of the day, no one or nothing will come between us, especially when people's lies go beyond the street.

CPSIA information can be obtained
at www.ICGtesting.com
Printed in the USA
LVOW09s0043110417

530296LV00014B/458/P

9 781544 107554